triscelle publishing

presents

# it's in the cards
## a lusty librarian adventure

### by

### heather poinsett dunbar
### & christopher dunbar

# acknowledgments

*Heather's Acknowledgments*

Wow… where did the time go. We wrote this originally about ten years ago after we finished what became Shards of Light and we wanted to write a fluffy romance tale. Mostly because we wanted to prove we could. This wouldn't be a stretch for two writers who managed to tell a strange story about mythical blood-drinking races. The two writers could see talented romance authors put together manuscripts quickly. If they can do this, why can't we, thought the two writers. Ha, ha, the fools mused, we can do that! No problem! The writing gods, in their infinite wisdom decided to show just how hard it can be to step outside one's comfort zone.

About a year later, we had finished a second draft and then real life started to throw curve balls. Layoffs occurred at jobs. Work began to involve three to four hours of a commute. Friends, family, and beloved pets passed on. The two writers, older and wiser (or so they thought) decided it was time to publish a novella that was originally supposed to be part of an anthology that we still hope will come together. In the end, thank you readers. Thanks to Ruth Davis Hays, who edited this again for us, and thank you to romance authors who make it look easy.

*Christopher's Acknowledgments*

Heather and I actually wrote this piece back in 2009 or 2010, but it has been sitting on our publication back-burner for several years. We had originally intended to release it as part of an anthology with other authors, but decided to release it on its own. However, it may yet be joined with other authors' stories.

After we finished the 1400-page manuscript that became Dark Alliance, Curse of Venus, and Shards of Light (three books in one manuscript… FYI, Morrigan's Brood and Crone of War were together one manuscript), Heather and I were so exhausted and teary-eyed that we decided to work on something fun. And so, Cheri and Algernon were born. Who would have thought that we would write a romance work together. Romance! You know, with a happy ending (not like our usually tragic or bitter-sweet endings).

Once we finished It's in the Cards, we went back to writing the Morrigan's Brood Series, starting with Odin's Chosen — we finished the manuscript — then Dynasties of Night —this manuscript is still incomplete, and we have sat on it for a few years. Today, we are working on a new series revolving around the Otherworld. I don't think we have a series name yet, but the titles include Dudes Love Pixies, Bitches Love Unicorns, and One Fat Witch.

Thank you Ruth and especially Heather on your work in bringing this title to fruition! Please enjoy this romp-filled tale!

# dedication and copyright page

## For Donna Rathbun

June, 2019

### It's in the Cards

A Lusty Librarian Adventure
Print ISBN-10: 1-937341-80-1
Print ISBN-13: 978-1-937341-80-0
by Heather Poinsett Dunbar
and Christopher Dunbar
Published by Triscelle Publishing
Edited by Ruth Davis Hays
Cover art arranged by Christopher Dunbar
Image ID: 75852505 (Section Breaks) Copyright Yuliia Pylypchuk | Dreamstime.com
Image ID: 77091256 (Chapter Breaks) Copyright Ildar Galeev | Dreamstime.com
Image ID: 5461454 (Back Cover) Copyright Alison Bowden | Dreamstime.com
Image ID: 9139608 (Front Cover) Copyright Igmit | Dreamstime.com
Image ID: 66107230 (Front Cover) Copyright Derek Tenhue | Dreamstime.com
All Dreamstime.com artists can be found on https://www.dreamstime.com/ on these
pages: yuliia25_info | flint01_info | alisonbowden_info | igmit_info | derektenhue_info
Triscelle Publishing Logo by Dayna Hartley

Visit our website, and find us on WordPress, Goodreads, Facebook, the Library Thing,
LinkedIn, Twitter, and many other places on the web.
www.triscellepublishing.com
triscellepublishing.wordpress.com

## Also available in several eBook formats

# chapter one

The smell of chemicals and dust made Cheri begin to cough once again. She blinked her itchy eyes and patted her pockets for her handy vial of anti-allergy eye drops.

"Damn," she whispered, realizing the bottle probably lay somewhere among the semi-useful odds and ends in the backseat of her Geo, along with gas station receipts, rain gear, gum wrappers, and a half dozen book bags, more or less.

Cheri shivered and rubbed her arms, giving up on the current preservation project in front of her. She sat in a messy lab room that remained at a constant temperature and humidity, surrounded by art supplies. Her back ached, but she loved her work in the rare book area at the university. Although she adored her advisor, she felt less like a doctoral student and more like free cheap labor for Dr. Reynolds.

An annoying ring made her jump, and she dropped the drying manuscript.

"Shit." Cheri ignored the phone for the moment, placed the drying parchment under weights, and began praying that the bath saved the aged document. She then opened the phone, not even bothering to examine the number. "Hello?"

"Hello, sweetie, it's your mother."

Cheri snorted. Her mother seemed to believe that Cheri forgot the sound of her voice between every phone call. "Hi mom, I'm kinda in the middle of something, now. Can I call you after work?"

"Oh, yes." Her mother's voice gained a somewhat disapproving tone. Her parents believed that she should be working in some financial field that involved making money, not spending her days with aged tomes and artifacts. "How are your projects going?"

"Quite well," Cheri explained. "I had to put the tarot project on hold, again. I'm waiting on the materials to arrive, so I'm working on preserving one of Benjamin Franklin's early works, and it's just made of some interesting paper that–"

"That's wonderful, dear. How is your money situation? Do you need groceries? Gas?"

Cheri closed her eyes. "Mom, I can live on the salary I'm getting from the university. You and dad should stop sending me money. It's embarrassing."

"I wish you'd stop voiding the checks we send," her mother answered. "There's nothing wrong with taking some help from your father and I. You could get your own home there." Cheri's mother stopped talking for a second. "But, I wasn't calling about money. I was wondering how busy your social schedule is."

Cheri frowned and rubbed her forehead. "I'm a bit too busy for dating, right now."

"Sweetie, you're over thirty. Perhaps it's time to find a man and settle down. You can keep working on this PhD of yours, but you can't wait forever. Don't you want children?"

Cheri bit her lip. "Not now," she admitted. "If I were interested in children, I'd start working in public libraries again."

"Do you remember Norman Bradley?" her mother asked.

"Normie?" Cheri groaned. "Norman Bradley III, right? The same boy who called me Four-eyes in grade and middle school? The one that would pop my bra and run off laughing about 'Cherry pop'? That pompous d…" Cheri paused, sparing her mother from her salty language. Her parents cussed a blue streak but were of the school of 'do as I say, not as I do'. "Yes, mom, I remember him. What about him?" A silence grew between herself and her mother. Cheri tapped her fingers against the tabletop.

"Well, you know how we kept in touch with the Bradleys, dear. Anyways, when we went to visit University Park last month on our vacation, we ran into him at his parents' home. Such a handsome young man, and he works as the IT guru for some securities company near where you work."

"That's nice, mom." Cheri rubbed her eyes, hoping that would be the end of this conversation.

"You and he should get together. Frankly, that roommate of yours and your other friends, well, they seem such a pack of–"

"Hippie bohemians?" Cheri chuckled, remembering what her father called the majority of her associates.

"Dear, it's time to grow up," her mother said. "Norman seems like such a nice guy. He's settled. I gave him your number," her mother's voice increased in tempo, "but I think he may be too bashful to call. You two need to get together and talk about memories and school. It'll be fun."

"Alright, mom. I'll call him, but I'm not promising anything!" Cheri knew if she didn't give in, her mother would continue needling her. Then the guilt would set in.

"Thank you, Cheri." She could almost hear her mother's smile in her voice. "Give him a call and tell him that we enjoyed spending time with him and his parents."

"Sure thing, mom." Cheri resumed scrutinizing the drying document.

As Cheri walked into the coffee shop, she brushed the white and gray cat hair off her dark green tunic blouse. She had a few nice things to wear, but most of them were destined for the cleaners, because Morty had decided they made the perfect bed and claimed them in the name of Catdom. The majority of her wardrobe was work related, clothes that could get messy, which meant her attire addressed the basic. The rest were her ancient 'date clothes'.

She stared down at the one nice skirt she owned and the pair of shoes that, in the last two years, had never left her closet, before walking up to the counter.

The barista leaned in and asked, "You want your usual?"

Cheri chuckled, drawn away from her garment analysis. "Sure, Dave, and one of the cookies I shouldn't eat."

Dave did his usual magic behind the counter and produced the delicacies she had ordered.

Cheri took her cookie and iced mocha and sat down on one of the overstuffed chairs. As she looked herself over in a dusty mirror across the room, she took in the rest of the coffee shop. Javaco did not look anything like a chain coffee shop. Old hardcover books served as decoration, furniture, and diversion. An enchanting blend of coffee, tea, and burning candles gave the outwardly nondescript shop some character. Decadent yet soft trance music cooed from an mp3 player.

Cheri sipped her drink and studied the other customers, trying to guess whether Norman had arrived yet, but no one looked her way. She caught her reflection again amongst the splotches in a vintage mirror and smoothed her frizzy hair down. She twisted a loose lock of her oddly-colored hair around her finger, annoyed that her topknot had come loose. Her hair shade tended to vary depending on the light. It moved from a strange hue of honey-gold to mouse brown to sorta reddish. She picked up her mocha and opened a well-worn copy of Pride and Prejudice.

When the door opened and a bell jingled, she glanced up to see the new customers. She spotted a dark and well-dressed figure enter the shop with a young, blonde woman accompanying him.

Cheri rolled her eyes a little.

*He has to be in his late thirties or possibly… nah, he is way too gorgeous and youthful to be in his forties.*

His broad shoulders and dark eyes caught her attention.

*He has to be at least six feet tall. Nice ass, too. However, his one fault lies with his choice of a girlfriend. Tan, blonde, limber, and young. Youth sucks!*

Cheri closed her eyes for a moment and licked her lips.

"Cheri?"

She looked up and stared at Norm.

*Yup, he hasn't changed much.*

Cheri stood and looked at Norm.

*Norm seems to be shorter than I remembered. Oh well, maybe it is due to the stupid heels I wedged on my feet.*

"Hey," she forced a grin onto her face. "Great to see you again, Norm."

He embraced her briefly.

She felt some relief that he didn't pop her bra, like the last time he hugged her.

"It's great to see you, too, Cheri," he answered, while running a hand through his dark blonde hair and smiling. Norman sat down across from her seat and set down his briefcase.

Cheri sat down and blurted out, "So, how's your family?" She tried to remember their names and faces.

"Oh, they're just fine," he said. "My older brother just got married. My little sister just had another baby." Norman's eyes started to dart around the room.

*It always seems distracting when he does this. It isn't lazy eye. Perhaps it is just a case of nerves.*

He continued talking. "My nephews and niece, they're very cute. They sort of remind me of you, very bookish. They never want to play. We're trying all sorts of physical activities with them, but Byron seems to be into reading the wizard, witch, and orc fantasy sort of stuff, and Maddie wants a pony. She rides, but we're trying to talk my sister into something like karate or something involving teams, but I've been having to travel for work quite a bit and…"

Cheri nodded her head, as Norm drawled on, and sipped her drink again. She then glanced over at the attractive man and the blonde girl as they sat down a few tables over. She noticed he wore tweed, and she could hear him over Norm, whose inane story of inconsequential current events faded to a mere whisper. Her jaw dropped a little as the man began to talk about the influence of Rome on Celtic culture.

"And we found evidence of an intermingling of Irish and Roman culture in Bath, of all places, Agnes! I mean… ten years ago, my advisor back then wouldn't let any of us even admit to there being a Roman influence in Ireland! Yet, we found evidence of a trading fort near the coast, and then we found artifacts from both cultures near this old Roman house in Bath. Now we get to exhibit what we found. First, a small display here with discoveries from other archeology sites from the golden age of the Celts, then it's on to Yale."

*He's English! Eeeeeee!*

His voice caressed her eavesdropping ears, and Cheri nearly sank to the floor. However, she couldn't hear the girl's reply.

Cheri looked back at Norman, glad she had managed to not blurt out her earlier rather embarrassing sentiment. She had an undeniable fascination for men from the British Isles and Ireland. It probably had something to do with kilts, her Celtic heritage, and the fact that she attended Cambridge for her undergraduate studies.

The intriguing mystery man didn't have a soft Londoner accent, though Cheri detected a hint of Scots as well as some Northern English dialect dotting his words. She felt as if she might melt into a puddle. Cheri looked at Norman, who didn't even seem to notice that her attention had waned.

He continued speaking as he looked around Javaco.

Her eyes darted back to the English guy, who must have said something amusing, as the girl giggled and covered her mouth.

The man smiled, but then he caught Cheri staring at him. His dark eyes fixed on her, revealing a moment of amusement. He grinned, in a rather impish fashion, but she witnessed a glimmer of sadness in those soulful eyes.

Then Cheri realized she was staring at the stranger and blushed, just in time for Norm's voice to regain her attention. Her eyes left the glamorous Englishman... Scotsman, or whatever, and settled on the dud sitting across from her.

"Yeah, I couldn't believe it either," Norman said, while leaning a little across the table. "I mean, telling me I couldn't be on the beach because I didn't want to take off my trunks. I mean… whatever happened to common decency and modesty? This is what happens when people start laughing at religion and decide to become socialists."

"Huh?" Cheri asked, feeling genuine confusion at how Norman moved from children's organized sports to nude beaches, religion, and politics.

"Sorry, I guess I jumped around on topics a bit." Norman smiled and leaned further toward her. "So, would you like to go to dinner with me? On a real date?"

Cheri clasped her hands together, careful not to bang her elbows on the table. She couldn't remember the last time she went on a 'real date'. At least Norman refrained from calling her 'Cherry Pop' or 'Cherry Bomb'.

*I could also try and help him learn that perhaps his problems… oh, who am I kidding, Norman would pay for our dinner. I would probably eat with the Fox News team, if they picked up the tab.*

Cheri snickered a little at that thought. "Sure, we can reminisce more then."

"Can you pick me up? My car is at the shop." Norman smiled at her.

"No prob," she answered.

Norm stared at his watch. "Well, I have to get back to the grind. I'm the only one at work that really writes the coding they need." He handed her a business card and stood up. "So, give me a call and we can catch up some more." Norman leaned over and kissed her cheek, leaving Cheri feeling a little disconcerted as he left Javaco.

She turned around and noticed the beautiful stranger and his girlfriend, Agnes, leaving.

*Dammit… no more sexy English accent.*

She sat down and re-opened Pride and Prejudice. "Why are accents so hot?" she whispered to herself, hoping nobody heard her.

◦◦◦◦◦◦◦◦◦◦

"Sophia, I'm home," Cheri shouted, hoping the call would be enough warning.

Sophia had said something earlier about a water leak at the dungeon and that a client might be loitering in their apartment.

Morty looked up from his couch, stared at her with the unimpressed glare of a feline emperor, and yawned. He then stood up, hopped down from his perch, and wandered over, winding around her legs upon arrival. After rubbing her, Morty received Cheri's proper demonstration of devotion. Then, he proceeded to lecture her on his requirements for more gooshy food.

"I fed you an hour ago, Mort," Sophia chastised as she wandered out of her room with a flogger in one hand and a pair of spike heels in the other. Her mundane everyday clothing bespoke little of her secret life. She scratched Morty's chin. "Honestly, you whine worse than some of my clientele." Cheri's roommate supplemented a rather small stipend from the university by working as a dominatrix at a dungeon. "How was The Norm?" She smirked at Cheri.

Cheri shrugged. "Everything my parents ever wanted in a boyfriend or possible fiancé."

"In other words, he's dull and best suited to be left behind," Sophia answered, before setting her things on an end table in the living room and sitting down on the couch.

Cheri shrugged again. "Norm asked me out on a real date."

"Please tell me you said no," Sophia bade.

"It's a free meal," Cheri admitted.

"So's the soup kitchen, but you aren't desperate enough to eat there," Sophia grumbled.

"I know," Cheri said, as she stood and walked into the kitchen. She grabbed a can of Morty's food from the pantry, opened the can, and scooped out the tender morsels into Morty's bowl. "But, I don't get asked out often," Cheri called out from the kitchen. "I think the last time someone asked me out was well over a year ago, around my thirty-second birthday."

Morty nearly knocked her over to get to his dish.

Sophia sighed audibly. "I don't think this is worth it, Cheri. You shouldn't rush anything in relationships when you feel this uncomfortable about it."

Cheri threw away the can, rinsed the spoon, deposited it in the sink, and walked out of the kitchen. "Who says I'm uncomfortable?"

Sophia raised a brow. "You looked more than a little glum when you mentioned he asked you out on a date."

Cheri plopped herself down with her back against the armrest on the opposite side of the couch and looked at her roommate. It was Cheri's turn to grumble. "This is what's wrong about rooming with a doctoral psych major. Stop trying to get into my brain. It's not that interesting, really. I promise."

Sophia stared at her. "I'd rather be single and somewhat lonely than married and miserable."

"It's just one date," Cheri replied, throwing up her hands. "Maybe he's just nervous and will become interesting and less conservative when I get a glass of wine in him."

"That's highly doubtful," Sophia said with a smirk, "but I have been wrong before, and you're allowed to go 'neener neener' at me. However, I get to do it too when he continues to be the dullest man on the face of the Earth." She stood up. "Well, I got invited to a play party, and somebody has to pay for these new toys. Don't spend all night watching the history documentaries. Oh, there's an idea. Take Normal to that Celtic exhibit at the university museum."

"Somehow, I don't think that will be an interest for him," Cheri countered. But then she remembered that the tweed hotness at Javaco mentioned something about the exhibit. "We'll see. Be careful."

"I always am," Sophia answered. "See you in the morning."

Cheri propped her chin against her open right palm and wondered if Norm had forgotten she was waiting for him. She'd spent most of yesterday afternoon cleaning out the car.

He hadn't seem all too thrilled with her date suggestions, so they decided to wait until they met up to make a final decision.

She jumped a bit, upon hearing a sudden knock on the window. She confirmed it was him who knocked and unlocked the door for him. "Hey," she said. "So, any thought on what to do tonight?" She smirked at him.

"I was thinking that maybe I need to let the lady choose," Norm answered as he sat down next to her. "If you have your heart set on the exhibit, we can go there after dinner, but I get to choose the restaurant."

Cheri grinned, pleased he wanted to compromise. "I'll go wherever you want to go for that."

"How about Italian?"

Cheri shrugged. "Pasta is always good."

"So, who exactly is this group?" Norman asked while motioning to a series of golden artifacts and jewelry.

"That's from the Iceni and Trinovantes," Cheri replied. "They were two neighboring tribes in Britannia in what is now London, or near London." She looked over the brochure. "Now, there's supposed to be some games and puzzles somewhere." She noticed Norm staring at a small, gilded, bare-breasted woman in a chariot and sighed. "How about we meet up in a half hour here. You can continue drooling over Boudicca, Medb, or the Morrigan," she commented before staring at the figure, trying to surmise whether the warrior woman wore a cloak of raven-feathers.

*That would be a sign that this could be a representation of Morrigan.*

Norm chuckled. "Sorry, sweetie, I got a little distracted. Honestly, I don't get this. Were all the women warriors in this culture?"

Cheri smiled again. "You know, in Celtic culture, the primary deities of battle, death, and war, were women. So, yes, there were a lot of women warriors, chieftains, and leaders in the Celtic and Briton tribes." Cheri frowned. "I wish I knew if it was right to lump the Picts, Gaels, Gauls, and Britons all together, but I suppose it's easy for an armchair historian to do so. Anyways..." She paused as she noticed how animated she had become, even though Norm looked a little bored. "Sorry, I'm just really passionate about this part of history. I love that we get to store the exhibits in the library for the History and Archeology Department. I'm dying to see the games they have stored. There's a rumor that there's a board game there." Cheri bounced a little.

"Oh, a board game," Norm commented. His eyes scanned the room. "I thought your mother said something about you working on something involving those witch cards."

Cheri grumbled to herself. "That's Tarot, Norm, and before people started using them to divine the future, people played games with them. I love the artwork on them, and preserving the cards and the artwork is important!"

Norm held up his hands. "Sorry, I just thought librarians read for a living. I assumed you spent most of your day telling stories to kids and shushing people."

"You sound like my parents." Cheri sat down on a bench. "I worked as a reference librarian before going back to work on my doctorate. I also worked as a research assistant while getting my master's. I was and still am an information retrieval expert and a knowledge junkie, not a day-care worker," she sighed. He looked a little confused. "Sorry," she apologized, "I get overly sensitive about my work, sometimes."

"So, will you go back to work at a library after you're done with your studies?" Norm asked.

"Well, not really," Cheri answered. "I liked my job, but I felt like I was an over-glorified computer technician most of the time. When I'm done, I'll probably work for a university in their Rare Books Department or at a museum. I may even decide to continue with more studies and get a doctorate in history or something. I love school."

"That doesn't seem useful." Norm's eyes turned sharp. "Why don't you get an MBA or go work for a law library?"

"You sound like my dad," Cheri groaned, trying to keep her cool. "I don't find law or managing people all that interesting. I like learning new things. It's what I'm good at."

"Well, what's the point of learning if you can't use it to make money?"

"Is that all you care about?" Cheri gave up on being calm. "What about enjoyment?"

"That's what hobbies are for," Norm countered. "You use a good education to get a good job, so you can afford hobbies to have fun."

Cheri felt a frown settle into her brow. "I have hobbies that are fun, but I don't use them to make up for feeling miserable at a job I would hate." In veiled disgust, she looked away from Norm, only to notice that the tweed hottie from the coffee shop and his girlfriend were watching them.

*Fine! I feel too much rage to remain unruffled.*

"Well, I suppose it doesn't matter much about your education if you plan to have kids," Norm stated.

Cheri fixed her gaze back on Norm. "Why? Wouldn't an education be of value if I have children?" she asked.

"Because, you'd be at home, taking care of the kids, cooking, cleaning, grocery shopping, that sort of thing," Norm deadpanned then shrugged. "You wouldn't have time for using your education."

"I see, I see…" Cheri saw red for a moment. "You think a woman's place is to be barefoot in the kitchen with a bun in the oven."

"That's not–"

Cheri stood up. "You obviously don't understand me, Norman. You see that woman driving the chariot? She's an equal… no, she's a superior in her world! I'd like to at least feel equal in my world, but because of attitudes like yours, women are regulated to being nothing more than housewives. I will never be a housewife! You and my parents seem to think that I'm only good enough for that! I don't want to see you again! Just take a fucking cab home. Go away and leave me alone."

The room erupted with clapping and cheering.

Cheri looked around, noticing many of the women in the museum smiling and cheering.

"You go, girl," a few women cried out.

Cheri ducked her head and darted for the doors. Even praise sometimes embarrassed her.

"I don't think this will work, mom," Norm muttered into his phone. "She's a weird book-worshipping nerd."

Norm's mom emitted a grumble of disapproval over the phone. "What did you do, call her 'Cherry Pop'? Admit that you spread that rumor about her in high school."

"No," Norm replied. "She's just really… opinionated, and I don't think she would ever get married."

"Nonsense," his mother cooed. "Every girl wants to get married. Just… you'll have to behave and fake an interest in her interests. Besides, it's a shame that a cute and rich girl like that is going to waste. Cheri needs to get married and grow up." His mother became silent. Then inhaled audibly. "Normie, she's not 'funny,' is she?"

Norm thought over that comment for a moment. "No, mom, she's not a lesbian. I don't think so, at least."

*Though, I have to admit to some doubts, at this point. What the fuck was with that women's lib speech?*

"Alright then," his mom said, "the best thing to do is apologize. Send her roses, surprise her at work. Send her poetry."

"I can't write that stuff," Norm replied.

"That's what the internet is for. You can find something romantic and send it to her. Maybe it's just a PMS thing." His mother sighed. "We need this. You know that."

Norm sighed back. "I know. Don't worry, mom."

# chapter two

**C**heri grumbled to herself before rescuing the pot of rice paste from the stove. She stuck it on a well-worn and particularly ancient pot holder that probably belonged to a long-gone grad student. She dumped some of the mixture into a Styrofoam cup. She then returned her attention to the clamshell box pieces and stirred the rice paste mixture again. The cold air of the lab caused her to shiver, so she pulled on the huge sweater and rubbed her hands together. Cheri decided to try to forget about that disastrous date and concentrate on work.

With her mind fixed on her work, Cheri stooped over the clamshells and began dabbing her paintbrush in the rice paste, wishing once again the new exhibits would arrive. She finished piecing together the box and turned on the timer, hoping the box would dry quickly in the cold and dry environment.

*Onto the next one.*

Cheri picked up another box and slid the sixteenth century copy of the Malleus Maleficarum within it. "Three down, four to go," she called out to the empty lab, feeling herself smile in relief. She then swiped at her brow.

*I could use a bit of a drink... too bad it is only water.*

She grabbed her bottle of water and took a sip.

*After the last clamshell is complete and dry, I will drop everything on Dr. Reynold's desk and read until the library closes. I hope the new collection shows up while I wait. A Victorian copy of the Marseilles Tarot doesn't arrive on loan every day.*

Just then, Cheri's cell phone buzzed, and she picked it up.

*Yet another text from Norm?*

She rubbed her forehead in annoyance.

*The man never gives up, apparently.*

"Never ever date a crazy," she muttered. "Or someone crazier than yourself." Cheri shoved her phone deep into her backpack to pretend it didn't exist. She wished she could change her phone number. As she lowered her head to the work table, she heard a buzz from the cell again. Then another, louder, ring echoed in the cold room.

*Great. What now? Can't they wait until I am done?!*

Cheri looked up from the work table. She then rubbed her hands and started to peel away the paste. "Just a minute! Keep your shirt on!" Cheri uttered a half-growl. In a fevered rush, she washed her hands and dried them impatiently on her skirt, noting again that they were still out of paper towels!

*I hope this means the tarot set has arrived, or someone is going to pay for interrupting me! Or they better have paper towels!*

Cheri dashed into the front room, grumbling at her paste-covered shoes. "Can I help–" she started to grumble, until she looked up into the eyes of the coffeeshop hottie. She noticed the backwards tag on his jacket and realized that he must work for the university.

"Hello…," she said in a more polite yet embarrassed tone. She could feel her cheeks blush.

"Hello," replied in that dreamy Scots-ish voice. He smiled at her, revealing a dimple.

"Uhm, can I help you?" Cheri stared into his eyes and felt herself start to fall into them. Beneath a lurking mischievousness, she witnessed a measure of sadness in their dark depths. She blinked, lost in his gaze.

"Pardon me," he began.

Now, she could sense nothing but his voice.

"I apologize for arriving so late," the hottie continued, "but I was hoping I could examine the artifacts from the Bath collection."

"Oh, the Bath collection," Cheri gulped.

*He's not the delivery I was expecting, but wow… the hottie's here! What do I do?*

"Are there any pieces that you specifically want to examine?" She hoped it would only be a few pieces. If he wanted more, she'd need a cart, not to mention help in loading and dragging the items to a table.

He pulled out a printout. "Specifically, I'd like to see B26 and D35."

Cheri felt a great deal of relief that he only wanted two items.

"I'll be right back," she informed him, hoping she didn't resemble the biggest idiot on campus. She walked into the storage room with her keys and unlocked the vault. Cheri then picked up two boxes and set them on the floor outside of the vault door. She closed and re-locked the vault, picked up the boxes, and set them on the table closest to him.

The hottie wore gloves and appeared to have all the supplies he needed ready to go.

Cheri unlocked the boxes and backed away from the table. She took a seat at another desk, hoping she didn't block his light, and watched him handle the exhibits. She fell silent as she watched him pull items from the cases.

"I'm sorry for bothering you once more," he said, revealing his dulcet and soothing voice again. "I need an extra set of hands with this. I'm having a bloody awful time getting this out. Can you assist?" He glanced up at her.

Cheri found her voice. "Of course."

She stood and walked over to the table before pulling on a pair of gloves.

As he held down the box, she noticed his tag move, revealing an 'A' for his first name, but little else.

Cheri pulled on the first item in the case, which felt like a wooden box surrounded in velvet, and managed to remove it successfully. She then placed it on the table and backed away again.

"Oh, this is so brill," he whispered, seemingly to himself. "Absolutely thrilling." He exhaled audibly and glanced at her again. "Have you ever seen one of these?"

Cheri took another look at the box, which appeared to have legs. "I don't know what it is," she admitted, hoping she didn't look as stupid as she felt at this point.

His mouth turned up, revealing a wicked and dazzling smile. "Are you sure you've gotten everything out of this case?"

Cheri moved back towards him again and pulled some more boxes out of the first case. "I'll let you examine this."

"No, please stay. This is the most extraordinary find of my career, and I would rather share the experience with someone rather than experience it alone," he stated. His eyes moved to hers again. "I'm afraid if I blink it will disappear on me," he chuckled. "Please share this with me." His voice revealed anxiety.

"Okay." Sheri smiled at him. "So, where did you find this?"

"My team and I found this at a site outside of Bath in England," he answered, "in what had been an old Roman house. It's a new museum, now, but we had no idea what treasures lay underneath until recently."

"So you're an archeologist?" Cheri rubbed her hands along the back of a chair.

"Yes," he answered. "Oh, forgive me for not introducing myself. I'm Algernon MacDonough." He smiled again, and the dimple reappeared.

"Oh, yes. I've heard of you," Cheri admitted, which wasn't a lie, as the entire university was whispering about this particular visiting professor. "I'm Cheri Tappan, hopefully PhD, one day." She noticed something in his eyes, revealing a desire to say more, but he returned to opening the box.

"We found a manuscript in the remains of an old monastery near Waterford, and there was mention of a fae treasure in Bath under a Roman villa. It gave some directions. We realized that the villa was this museum. We dug and found baths, catacombs, and several vaults. Most were empty. However, one contained a trove of artifacts. Many of the pieces are interesting and rather controversial. They may very well redefine what we understand about the ancient world."

Cheri leaned forward and tried not to look too excited. "In what way?"

*I feel like such a history nerd. This is so exciting!*

Dr. MacDonough continued unwrapping the box. "Let me finish setting this up, and it will become evident."

Cheri watched him place a solid wooden board with circular legs in the middle of the table. Celtic knotwork and Roman key patterns decorated the board and intertwined. Inlaid silver ornamented the wooden board. She noticed a series of holes in the top of the board. The wood's finish seemed quite intact and polished for a piece of this age.

Dr. MacDonough began opening the other boxes and extracted a series of small wooden figures decorated in colorful paint and silver, each wielding a small weapon. He placed them in the holes in the board.

"I know what this is," Cheri gasped. She could see a gleam in the archeologist's eyes. "Is it a Fidell board?" she asked.

Dr. MacDonough smiled. "Close, Ms. Tappan, it's actually pronounced 'fickle', however the spelling is misleading, as it's spelled close to your pronunciation, f-i-d-c-h-e-l-l." He looked at her and asked, "So you know something about it?"

"I know it's supposed to be like a Celtic version of Chess, but that's probably somewhat inaccurate," Cheri admitted. She studied his broad shoulders again.

"It actually predates Chess and most other board games. However, you're quite right about its origins." He put the last game piece into the middle hole. "Voilà."

Cheri started re-examining the board and noticed that the inside team of game pieces held short swords, surrounding a well-dressed piece in the center adorned with a colorful red helm. Red paint decorated the other pieces surrounding him. However, the outside pieces wielded longer swords, wore silver torcs, and had painted facial hair. They even looked to be painted in a Celtic style. She glanced back at Dr. MacDonough. "This depicts Romans and Irish Gaels?" she whispered in shock.

The archeologist clapped. "Well done. It took my team months to reach that conclusion. They were convinced it was Vercingetorix. How did you know it was Irish?"

Cheri felt her cheeks redden. "Well, we have a tarot deck in the collection where the artist combined artwork from the Book of the Kells and from Newgrange, and it seems similar. It was just a guess." She shrugged.

"Well, your guess is bang-on," Dr. MacDonough murmured. He then scratched at the day of beard growth on his chin.

Cheri felt if she might start glowing. "How do you play it?"

He smiled, revealing teeth.

*God, he even had beautiful teeth.*

"I'm so glad you asked. Pull up a chair." Dr. MacDonough oriented the board so they could both reach it. While he talked, Cheri grabbed a chair from the other desk and set it down at the table. "It's a game of strategy, tactics, guile, and fun. In a modern fidchell set, you have a chieftain-king in the center of the board with his personal guard–"

"So," Cheri interrupted after sitting down, giddy, "since these inner pieces are Roman soldiers, then the most interior piece is the Emperor? I'm sorry, I got excited," she admitted.

"No, please continue," Dr. MacDonough said. He sat down across from her.

"However, since these pieces aren't purple, they aren't the Emperor's Praetorian guard, so this is most likely a Roman general," Cheri mused aloud.

"Brilliant, Ms. Tappan, well done." Dr. MacDonough answered. "The outer pieces in modern sets are assassins. Their job is to surround and kill the king."

"I suppose," Cheri reasoned. "Since these are Irish warriors, they are in direct conflict with the Romans and are trying to kill the general." She decided that she needed to tell him to stop calling her by her last name soon.

"Yes," Dr. MacDonough said. As he leaned in closer, his dark eyes revealed a growing spark of interest. "This is the unique thing about this set. None of our records show a force of Romans in conflict with a force of Irish warriors. They traded at a post near the coast, but we have no records of an invasion or military conflict. The Irish would never keep a written record of such a thing, but the Romans would have. Had there been a conflict, every historian would have mentioned it. Yet, we have nothing."

Cheri nodded. Though this line of speculation seemed interesting to her, she felt like competing against this dreamy, intelligent man. "So how do we play fidchell?"

"The objective of the Roman soldiers is for the general to escape by reaching one of the four corners. The Irish warriors will try to surround him on all four sides." Dr. MacDonough leaned back in his seat. "Like in every conflict, there are causalities."

"How do the pieces move?" Cheri asked.

"We take turns. The pieces move like rooks do in a straight line. However, unlike rooks, they cannot take an enemy piece on their own."

Cheri leaned forward as he continued explaining the finer points of the game.

*I like him. I really like him. Now I am going to beat him at his own game! Or not. Just to play this fascinating game against a man like him will be fun!*

"Well that was close. Very close," Algernon admitted. He looked over at Cheri. "Did you enjoy the game?"

*The Roman general escaped by his teeth in this round.*

Cheri pushed her reddish hair behind her ears. "Oh, yes." She smiled. "It was difficult to understand at first, but I think I got it."

"Yes, it requires more thought than one would think," he replied, hoping this would not lead to a long silence. Algernon picked up a few of the remaining pieces on the board and began to box them.

"Is this the only way to play it?" Cheri asked.

"Oh no, there are several variations we have learned about, but we don't know when they originated," he admitted.

"So, when do you believe this was made?" Cheri stood up and dusted off her skirt.

He tried to not stare at her legs. "We carbon dated it, and it looks like it was made in the eighth century."

Cheri's eyes grew wider. "Eighth century? It's that modern? Why wouldn't they make a set with Charlemagne and the Saxons in that era?" Cheri picked up the two remaining pieces on the board and held them up to the light. "If someone was making a fidchell set, would they use the wood from the same tree?"

"Yes," he answered, "although, if someone had to make a spare piece, it would come from different wood."

"Have you run tests on the wood to see where it came from?"

Algernon felt a tinge of embarrassment. "No, not yet," he admitted. "It's an excellent recommendation. The collection has other pieces, and we had to investigate those first."

*Cheri is obviously quite brilliant.*

She extended the two pieces back to him.

He took her hand and held it for a moment, feeling her warmth radiate through the gloves. Algernon stared at her, though her face seemed unreadable, and he felt like a first class git.

*She is probably back with the arsehead from the museum and coffeeshop.*

He dropped her hand and began packing up the pieces.

*Best to pretend there was no touching.*

"Could you help me with this?" Algernon asked after looking back at Cheri, hoping he could gage her reactions. He watched her smile again, her full lips turned up.

"No problem," she said. Cheri then picked up the fidchell board and looked at the other side of it. "Wait." Her voice rose. "Did you see the writing under the board?"

"Yes." Algernon looked up from the boxes with the pieces.

"'Marcus Galerius Primus Helvetticus'? Are you sure about the carbon dating? I mean, why would someone in the eighth century have a full Roman name, including a Cognomina ex virtute?"

"I have no idea," Algernon replied. "I mean, that was not the practice then. Most people were known as 'name of birthplace'."

Cheri studied the board again, pursing her mouth in a most attractive manner. "Alright, let's assume for the moment that the carbon dating may be incorrect." She looked over at Algernon, and he realized her eyes were a lovely hazel.

"Alright." He closed up the boxes of the combatant pieces.

"Were… if this name is the name of the owner of this fidchell set, and it's truly his name, and used properly…" Cheri sucked in some air. "Helvetticus would mean that this individual distinguished himself in battle against the Helvetti."

"So that would be 58 BCE, when he would have been given the Cognomina ex virtute of Helvetticus," Algernon surmised.

"So, were fidchell boards popular in the Roman Republic?" Cheri asked.

"Oh no!" Algernon chuckled a little at the thought of that. "Definitely not, because only the barbarians in Éire and Britannia would have them."

"So, a Roman soldier from 58 BCE owned a fidchell board from Britannia or Ireland with Roman and Irish figures and Roman and Celtic art, but the carbon dating says this came from the eighth century."

Algernon shrugged. "Yes, that's correct."

"That is an incredible mystery," Cheri murmured.

Algernon smiled as he finished closing up the fidchell board. "If you think that's a mystery, you should see this," he suggested. "We found this cup along with the board. We carbon dated it to the sixth century." As he spoke, Algernon pulled the silvery bronzed cup from its box and held it up for Cheri to see before handing it to her. "When and where do you think this was made?" he asked her.

"With the knotwork, I'd say Ireland, Scotland, Wales, or the kingdom of Dalriada," she answered, taking it from him.

"That is what the tests revealed to us. However, to deepen the mystery, turn it around."

Cheri turned it and studied the inscription. "I don't understand this language," she admitted, "but I see two names. I think the first is Máire. The second is Marcus Galerius Primus Helvetticus. And this is sixth century?" Cheri sounded excited. "This has to be a coincidence."

"That still isn't all," Algernon stated. "First, the words you couldn't read say 'to Máire Ní Conghal from Marcus Galerius Primus Helvetticus'. Then there is the typical Gaelic blessing along the lines of 'may this cup help you celebrate much happiness…sláinte chugat'. That means, to your health." He paused for a moment. "Not only was this Celtic drinking vessel given as a gift from a person with a Roman name to an Irish woman, but also no woman in the sixth century would dare call herself 'Máire'."

Cheri studied the cup more. "Doesn't that mean something like Mary?"

"Bang on," he said. "In this historical period, it would be considered blasphemous to take the name of the Holy Mother. If a child was named in honor of Mary, they would be called 'Maél Muire'. However, there are sources that say Máire means something like 'greatly desired' or even 'bitterly wanted'. Perhaps it's a nickname."

"That doesn't make sense at all. I mean, a woman having a name that is considered in poor taste for the time," Cheri commented, before passing him the cup.

"This is why these artifacts intrigue me," Algernon said. "If this Marcus Galerius Primus Helvetticus is the same person…" He then noted Cheri's skepticism etched in her face. "For arguments' sake. Here, we have a name that was given in 58 BCE. This name appears on an Irish drinking vessel from the sixth century and on a fidchell board from the eighth century." Algernon packed up the cup and shook his head. "It's fascinating isn't it?" He noticed Cheri appeared to be lost in thought.

"Marcus Galerius Primus Helvetticus," she whispered again. "I think I've seen that name before."

His heart skipped a beat. "You have?"

"I think so. Yes! Are you done looking at these? There's a book we need to see, but I have to finish here first."

Algernon felt his curiosity grow at her excitement. Then he decided that this would be an excuse to spend more time with her. "Yes, I'm done for now." He began helping her with the cart.

"Wait right here. I'll be back." She turned and raced the cart to the other room. A scant few seconds later, Cheri arrived and grabbed his hand.

As he followed her, he sensed growing passion within her.

Cheri's hair began to fall loose to drape past her shoulders.

He felt his desire for her grow.

"There's a history of the end of the Roman republic by a historian named Claudius Flavius," Cheri explained as she gasped for breath. "We have a translation of his work from the nineteenth century by Sir Edward Cunningham. It's in another storage room." Cheri fumbled for her keys as they reached the door. She unlocked it, turned on the lights, and pulled him inside. She began to open cabinets, all the while watching her breath in this cold room. Cheri didn't seem to realize her chest heaved a little.

Algernon closed his eyes, willing himself to calm a bit, not only about the excitement of discovering something new about his find, but also of being this close to such a beautiful, intelligent, and engaging woman.

She crouched down and reached into one of the cabinets, removing one of the boxes. She then opened the box and removed the book within. After setting it down on a table, she began to skim the pages with a great deal of care. "Here! Here it is!"

Algernon leaned in and then realized they were cheek to cheek, now. He tried to focus on the book, but her warmth distracted him from the text. "General Marcus Galerius Primus Helvetticus traveled with General Gaius Julius Caesar and the seventh and tenth legions during the first invasion of Britannia," he began to read aloud. "Galerius left on a mission to retrieve further supplies and reinforcements from the western side of Britannia. Only Mandubratius, the self-proclaimed chieftain of the Trinovantes, survived this mission. Mandubratius fought alongside Caesar until dying at the Battle of Pharsalus."

"Isn't this amazing?" Cheri turned towards him, her face a few inches from his. Her bliss-filled eyes revealed a growing fervor. Her breath disclosed a budding sweetness.

*I can no longer think. I hope she doesn't mind if I move first.*

Algernon pulled Cheri towards him.

Her lips parted slightly as his mouth pressed against hers.

He moved his arms around her and pulled her closer.

She responded with an eagerness that he had not expected. Cheri suckled at his lips, as her hands slid through his hair.

Algernon opened his mouth, and her tongue caressed his. A growing erection distracted him from any other thought. He moved his hands to her hips. He then pushed Cheri to the desk and lifted her butt to the top of it. He slid his hands under her skirt and fondled her bare skin. He felt a split second of shock as one of her hands began stroking him through his pants. He felt her begin to unfasten his belt. He glanced down at her, in something of a daze, and saw that her eyes remained shut. He ground himself into her hand as the intense kisses continued.

This entire scenario moved so quickly, but he couldn't help himself, and Cheri seemed lost in her excitement as well.

Algernon slid his fingers through the sides of her panties.

Just then, the bell rang, and Cheri pulled away. He wondered if he looked half as frustrated as she did.

Cheri felt like she might scream in rage.

*This has been my first passionate encounter in about, EVER!*

She sighed as Dr. MacDonough backed off a little, though his warm hands remained on her hips and under her panties. She also wondered where their gloves went. She uttered a frustrated sound and motioned for Dr. MacDonough to move behind the desk next to them.

Sadly, she felt his warm hands pull away from her sides, and she felt a greater deal of annoyance at having to miss more. She stood up and straightened her skirt and sweater.

The doorbell pealed again.

"Coming," she yelled, before snorting at the irony of that statement. Cheri began fumbling for her keys and finally saw them on her cart.

Dr. MacDonough tossed them to her.

Cheri felt a moment of shock that she managed to catch them. "Be quiet. Don't touch anything," she whispered, trying to sound stern.

He nodded and appeared to suppress a smile.

She turned back and smoothed her hair again, and then she headed for the main room. As Cheri approached the front door of the rare books offices, she whispered to herself, "I'm a librarian, not a sex-starved college student." She opened the door and stared at the delivery man. "Hi, Barry, what do you have for me?"

*Good, calm, cool, collected.*

Barry grinned and held out the box. "More cards, I'm guessing. So, what took you so long?" he asked, raised a brow in apparent intrigue.

"I was looking over some delicate parchment, and it took awhile to put it away." She hoped she still looked serene.

"Well, see you tomorrow. Don't stay out here too late." Barry then left the office and started pushing his cart of boxes again.

"Good night," she called out, before closing the door. She heaved a sigh of relief. Once Barry was gone, Cheri called out, "You can come out now."

The store room door opened, and Dr. MacDonough peered out around the corner.

She chuckled a little and motioned him forward

He smirked at her and approached her as if to embrace her again, but Cheri held up a hand and inclined her head towards a small camera.

"Sorry. These cameras are monitored and recorded."

"Then, let's go back into the store room and look over that book again," he murmured in a husky voice.

*Damn my insane accent lust!*

"I wish I could," she admitted, "but I've got to look over this new deck and catalog it." She patted the box.

"New deck?"

"Yes, it's a tarot deck. It's sorta another interest of mine. I like the artwork and history," she said with a shrug. Part of her waited to hear a reaction like the ones she heard from her parents and Norm.

"Alright, then. Let's take a look at it together. It's been a long time since I catalogued anything."

Cheri tried to keep from smiling too much. "Great, but you have to promise not to be a distraction, and you have to do what I tell you, Dr. MacDonough."

A smile lit his entire face, and his eyes seemed to lose their earlier sadness. "Call me Algernon," he said. "Just don't call me Al, or Algie."

Cheri chuckled a little. "Then call me Cheri, but don't call me Cherry. Let's get back to work. Grab that box of gloves, Algernon."

# chapter three

heri stopped in the parking lot and let *Nessum Dorma* wash over her with its timeless beauty, a fitting end to a night of fun. She inhaled thinking how wonderful Algernon had been. A moment of worry flashed in her mind.

*What if he is in a relationship with someone else? Like that girl he was with?*

She hated the thought of being the other woman. However, she forgot that concern when his sexy brains overwhelmed her. His exterior and that accent were hot enough, but add his intelligence and she couldn't help herself.

Things almost started again in the middle of cataloging, but then a phone call had interrupted them. Algernon had to leave, though he promised to meet with her again.

Cheri closed her eyes, wondering when he would come back into her life, when a fierce knocking at the driver's side window made her jump.

*Norm? What does he want?*

Cheri considered driving away, but she had to tell Sophia about this evening, which meant she needed to get around Norm. She rolled down the window, annoyed at the idea of seeing him again. He appeared to still be dressed in his work clothes. "What?" Cheri growled.

"Where have you been?"

"That's none of your business!"

"But you haven't returned my calls." Norm leaned in closer to the open window.

"I was busy. I joined a cult of cannibals, and we're joining forces to battle zombies in Budapest," Cheri answered, pleased with her smartassed remark.

"I've been waiting here for hours. Don't you know how dangerous it is out here, Cheri?" He leaned in close enough for his tie to drape over the electric window.

Cheri grabbed his tie, keeping her grip strong, and pulled him even closer. She began raising the window with her left hand.

"What are you doing? Stop!"

She ignored his protests as she locked the doors and finished rolling up the window. Cheri then began scooting over to the passenger side of her car.

Norman pulled at the door latch, but the locked door wouldn't open.

Cheri pulled up the lock on the passenger door and opened it. After scooting out, she locked it and closed it, all the while ignoring Norm. She wondered how long it would take for him to figure out that he could get out of the trap by untying the knot of his tie.

Without even a glance back, she walked into the apartment and found Sophia sitting on the couch next to a stranger playing her game console. There appeared to be a lot of shooting coming from the game. Cheri looked out the window and noticed that nobody appeared to be helping Norm. She then went to the kitchen and grabbed a bottle of hard cider from the fridge and began drinking.

"Cheri?" Sophia called out.

Cheri walked back into the living room to find Sophia looking at her from the couch.

"I didn't even hear you come in," Sophia said while holding up a game controller. "Wanna join in?"

"Meh, I suck at those games," Cheri said before chuckling. Upon catching Morty in the chair, Cheri scratched his chin. She eyed the young man and asked, "So, who's this?"

"Oh… crap," Sophia muttered, as her character bit the dust. "I was so close to getting the next crown, too." Continuing to play, she looked over at Cheri and beamed. "You are glowing, girl!"

The stranger finally turned towards Cheri. "I'm Scott."

Sophia raised a brow at Cheri. "Yes, this is Scott."

"S'up?" Scott uttered, before taking a sip of a beer.

"Not much." Cheri chuckled again.

"Us girls gotta take a tinkle, Scott," a suddenly animated Sophia announced before grabbing Cheri's arm and pulling her towards the bathroom.

"Okay," Scott deadpanned as he started the game again.

Sophia pushed Cheri into the bathroom. "What happened?"

Cheri shrugged. "You tell me first. Who's the videogame geek?"

"He's my latest experiment," Sophia admitted.

"Experiment?"

"I wanted to see what nerds and geeks were like. So far, this has been a pleasant surprise." Sophia smirked. "Now, will you tell me why you're glowing?"

Cheri leaned against the sink counter and recalled the evening. She felt her body flush as the remembered her emotions, from giddy to guilt and then lust. Then, there was Norm. "I'm in lust," she admitted to Sophia.

"Lust, not love?"

"Well, I don't know him well enough for that." Cheri felt her face widen in a big smile. "However, the lust is there."

"Who? Please don't let it be that worm, Norm."

"Oh, no way, ick. He's been stalking me, and I'm tired of it."

"That's horrible." Sophia's large brown eyes reflected pity then returned to curiosity. "If Norm's not your loverboy, then who is?"

"He's no boy," Cheri blurted and then chuckled. "He's a man."

Sophia inhaled. "So, this man is older?"

"And wiser," Cheri added. She watched her friend make a bit of a face. "Oh, he's not that old!"

"He's not married, is he?"

Cheri exhaled. "Give me some credit, Sophia. I wouldn't do that." She bit her lip. "At least, I don't think so. No wedding ring. No indentation on his finger. He may have a girlfriend, though." Cheri placed a hand over her forehead. "Oh, Sophia, what am I gonna do?"

"So, what happened?"

Cheri studied the concern in Sophia's face. "Well, I was waiting for another tarot set when he showed up. I pulled some artifacts out for him, and we started talking about them and getting into some really interesting historical stuff, and then he kissed me, and I sorta encouraged him. Next thing I knew… well, I unfastened his belt and his hands were under my skirt–"

Sophia raised a brow again. "Did you–?"

"No," Cheri interrupted Sophia. "The tarot set arrived, and then we started cataloging it together." She grinned again. "Then he got a phone call and had to leave."

Sophia smirked. "It sounds like you really like him. Do you know his name?"

"Yes," Cheri admitted. "He's Algernon MacDonough from Cambridge."

Sophia's smile faded. "Are you out of your mind, dating a professor?"

"Well, he's not mine!"

Sophia sighed and leaned against the sink counter. "I think I met him at a welcome to our visiting and new faculty party. He was there with his niece. I'm teaching her social psych class."

"Niece?" Cheri asked. "What does she look like?"

"Oh, the usual white college girl." Sophia shrugged. "Blonde hair, blue eyes, thin, a rack Scott would kill for, I bet." Sophia chuckled again.

"I thought they were dating," Cheri admitted.

"Ewww. Where did you see them?"

"The museum and Javaco."

Sophia started laughing. "Cheri, nobody takes a date to the museum!"

"But you told me to take Norm there."

"Yeah, because he's just not right for you." Sophia shrugged. "I figured he'd feel stupid there and get tired of it. So, why Dr. MacHottie? Why not another student?"

"All the male students my age are married, in a relationship, gay, or just want in my pants," Cheri said.

"And so does Dr. MacHottie," Sophia argued.

"Well, I think he likes my brain, too. What if he's married, though?"

Sophia stopped leaning against the sink. "No, he's not married."

"How do you know?" Cheri asked.

"I know from the party. He and I were talking, and he told me his wife died of pancreatic cancer about five years ago. He said that he was tired of avoiding life and had decided to venture forth out of the UK."

Cheri felt a twinge of jealousy. "How do you know so much about him?"

Sophia chuckled. "Girl, I'm a student of human nature. Everyone tells me this kind of stuff because I'm a good listener... even you tell me everything, or almost everything."

A knock interrupted Sophia.

"I gotta use the can," Scott called out through the closed door. "You two can make out some other time."

"Make out?" Cheri snorted.

Sophia opened the door and then Scott pushed past them.

At that moment, the phone began to ring, and Cheri raced over to pick it up. "Hello?" She wondered if Algernon had found her phone number.

"How could you drag Normie to a museum exhibit? What did you expect?"

"Hi, mom," Cheri muttered, rubbing her forehead. "Look, I don't do nightclubs, there weren't any movies out I wanted to see, and he got to pick the restaurant, which sucked, by the way. What about what I want to do?"

"You won't find a nice boy if you're just thinking about what you want to do," her mother said with a bit of a huff. "He can provide for you, and he already likes you. How could you forget how much time you spent together growing up?"

"Well, he may have been a nice kid, but now he's acting like a jackass," Cheri argued. "I'm not interested in him anyways."

"Nonsense. Your father and I are sending you tickets to fly home and visit us. You two can patch things up on the way."

"I have to–"

"First-class seats."

"Next to each other?" Cheri groaned. "I have work."

"I talked to your advisor. She said you deserved a long weekend."

"Mom! I can't believe you did that! I'll be a laughingstock!"

She heard a snort from her mother. "You can at least show some gratitude, pumpkin."

Cheri sighed.

*Mom wields guilt as a skillful artist might wield a paintbrush.*

"I'm sorry, mom. It's just that I'm sorta seeing someone."

Her mother chuckled. "You're a horrible liar, Cheri. We just want you happy, pumpkin. See you next weekend. Bye, bye."

Cheri winced hearing her mother blow kisses over the phone line before hanging up on her.

"Let's change the phone number," she muttered to Sophia, who listened in throughout the entire conversation by holding her head close to Cheri's.

"At least your mom and dad care," Sophia commented. "So, what will you do about Dr. MacHotstuff?"

"Uhmmmm…"

The doorbell rang, and Cheri stalked towards it, half-expecting to see Norm standing there without a tie. She peered through the eyehole and saw nothing. She opened the door, hoping he wouldn't jump from behind the corner. Cheri peeked out and then noticed an envelope, with her name printed on the front of it, taped to her door. She pulled it off and wandered back in before Morty could decide to attempt an escape. Opening the envelope, she pulled out a beautiful tarot card of The Fool and a short note. She smiled.

Sophia then yanked the cards and envelope from Cheri, to which Cheri responded, "Hey!"

"Well, well, well," her roommate mused. "'I'm so sorry our time was cut short, my honey'." She began muttering to herself, while reading the included poem, and grinned. "Oooo, very nice. Gotta love a man who can spin poetry."

Cheri tried to grab the card, but Sophia pushed away Cheri's hands and sniffed the card.

"And one who smells good, too," Sophia added. "Musk and blood orange if I'm not mistaken." She giggled.

Cheri this time managed to successfully yank the envelope back from Sophia. "How do you know scents so well," she asked.

Sophia shrugged. "Just a hobby. So, no name on the card. Who do you think sent it? Maybe Norm was trying to make it up to you. Though, if that's the case, he's more into brainy girls than I would have thought."

"Oh please," Cheri chuckled. "Who do you think sent this? My honey? Nobody says that here... stateside. Besides, Norm isn't into smart girls."

Sophia raised a brow. "How is it you never talked about this leech before?" She sat down and patted the next seat cushion.

Cheri gave in and sat on the couch. "I try to forget somewhat unpleasant memories," she admitted. "We had fun growing up together, but around middle school, Norm decided 'man' equaled 'in charge' and I should just defer to him in, well, everything. My parents thought we should date, so I gave in to them, and peer pressure, and went to prom with him." Cheri felt her nose wrinkle in annoyance at the memories. "Let's just say he wasn't a gentleman, and I thought he may have grown up by this point. Apparently, I was sort of the trophy girl, maybe..." Cheri paused in contemplation. "My parents are well off. His weren't so much, but were ambitious, and my parents sorta like suck-ups. My parents are nice, in their way," she sighed. "But, they just are into appearances too much." As Cheri rubbed her forehead, Morty crawled into her lap.

"So, what happened after high school?" Sophia asked, crossing her legs.

"He went to a state university, and I went to Cambridge."

Sophia slammed a fist against the couch.

Mort looked up at the sudden movement.

"Holy shit! How did I not know this?"

Cheri shrugged. "It's not really a big deal. My parents wanted me to go to some private university, and I agreed, but only if I got to go to Cambridge. It has a great History Department."

"Why did you wind up at a hellhole like Penton?"

Cheri chuckled. "Dr. Reynolds taught my Rare Books and Special Collections classes at NTU, where I got my Masters. She came over here to assist with their collections, which were in dire need of preservation, and to help with the university's Library Science program, which sucks but can be improved on. So, I came with her. I wanted to pay for my own schooling, but I couldn't afford Cambridge on my own. My parents aren't really into the whole postgraduate education deal. I think they were hoping that I'd settle down, or just settle."

"Wow." Sophia sat back, her eyes narrowing. "Hey, Professor MacFinetush is from Cambridge. Did you and he–?"

Cheri felt her mouth open. "No! I didn't know him, then. Cambridge isn't small, you know. Besides, he was probably married, back then." She began to wonder if she did know him or might have seen him there, but then Scott interrupted her thoughts as he strolled into the living room.

"Did you turn on the fart fan?" Sophia asked.

Scott reddened for a moment. "I will," he muttered, before heading back for the bathroom. He looked over his shoulder at Cheri. "You wanna play, too?"

"Sure," she said, picking up the third controller, as Scott ambled towards the back of the apartment.

"While gamers are creative in bed, they lack social graces," Sophia admitted with a smirk.

Cheri pondered on the other news she needed to tell Sophia, but her memory failed her on whatever that might be.

*It can wait.*

⬛▦▦▦▦▦▦▦═══╱▦▦▦▦▦▦▦═══╱▦▦

*This situation is intolerable! How could she leave me like this?!*

Norm spent several minutes trying to tug the knot out of his tie, but it remained in place. He tried looping a finger in the tie to get more room, but it grew tighter, gagging him a bit. Then he heard footsteps and turned his head, as best as he could, to see a mother walking her baby in a stroller. "Can you help me, ma'am?" he called out. "Please!"

The woman snorted. "Why don't you just untie it," she asked.

"I can't leave my tie," he insisted.

The sound of spinning wheels on the road heralded the arrival of some teenagers skateboarding across the street. One of them said to his buddies, "I bet he locked his keys in the car."

"What a dork," another shouted out, before the group erupted in chuckling.

Norm was about to say something else when he heard a radio squawk, as a squad car pulled up with its lights flashing.

A female officer stepped out of her car, walked over to him, and stared into his eyes. From his crouched position, she resembled an Amazonian warrior.

"Good… evening, officer," he squeaked.

"Sir, is this your vehicle?"

"I can explain," he began, trying to see past the sunglasses.

"Yes or no, is this your vehicle?" Her voice yielded little emotion.

"Uhm, no."

The officer turned and spoke into her radio. "Unit 23, I have a 62C in progress, about to take suspect into custody."

A crackle of static echoed around them for a moment. "10-4, 23. Do you need backup?"

"Wait!!!!"

The officer glared back at him. "Speak when spoken to," she ordered in a firm tone. The officer then turned back to her radio. "Not at this time. Will advise."

"10-4, 23."

The officer turned back towards Norm and pulled a set of handcuffs out of a pouch.

"Please, that's not necessary."

The officer stared at him for a moment, and Norm lowered his eyes. "Get on your knees and reach for the roof," she ordered.

Norm closed his eyes for a second.

*Just what I need... a criminal record.*

As he followed her directions, he felt her move behind him and cuff him. He sensed her double-lock the cuffs.

"Can you stand?"

"No, ma'am, my tie isn't long enough," Norm admitted.

"Sir, are you comfortable in this position," she asked.

"I don't know how I can get comfortable," he answered.

"If you promise not to move, I'll help you."

He mused on how not moving could lead to comfort, but he decided to stay still. "I promise."

He heard a noise and witnessed a shiny blade a few inches from his face. The knife sliced through his tie, and Norm felt himself fall backwards, but a strong hand held him steady.

"Okay," the officer began. "Lift up your right foot and put it down in front of you."

He did as she ordered.

"Now stand."

Blood began circulating in his legs again as he rose, but they weren't sturdy enough to hold him up, so he fell against Cheri's car.

"I'm sorry!" he said. "I'm just a little weak."

"How long have you been here like this?" the officer asked.

"Over half an hour," he admitted.

As the officer escorted him to the patrol car, all he could think about was how he'd wind up being someone's bitch after the first night.

"What's your name?"

"Hu... Norman Bradley III," he answered. "My identification is in my right pants pocket," he added.

*Maybe being helpful will turn this into a warning.*

She fished his wallet out after scrutinizing him. "Do you know why I handcuffed you, Mr. Bradley?"

Norm looked at her. "No, ma'am."

*If we weren't in this situation, I'd be turned on. The officer is definitely a hottie.*

"I handcuffed you and will be arresting you for attempted auto theft."

"Attempted auto theft," he yelped. "I wasn't trying to steal Cherry's car!"

"Cherry?"

Norm sighed. "Cheri Tappan. She's a friend of mine."

"So, why are you breaking into a friend's car," the officer asked.

"I wasn't breaking in… can I explain, please?"

"Very well."

"I'd come up to her to apologize for being a jerk," Norm stated, "but we had another argument, and she grabbed my tie and rolled up the window."

The woman shifted her weight and scanned the apartments. "Where does Cheri live?"

"In apartment 114."

The officer wrote down something in her notepad. "I'll check out your story, but you'll have to sit in the squad car." She then opened the door, helped him in, and closed the door.

Norm turned his head and looked in bewilderment and embarrassment over the gathered crowd, especially the woman with the stroller and the skateboarders, who laughed into their hands.

*Will Cheri back me up? If not, I will wind up in jail for the night. Then there could be state or federal prison.*

Norm shuddered at the thought. After several minutes waiting, he heard a door close and looked up. The officer walked towards her cruiser and appeared to be smiling, but when she noticed him in the car, her smile faded. She reached the car, looked him over again, and opened the door.

Norm could see her name now, S. Lisle.

Officer Lisle tugged him out and took him to the front of the car. She then began to unfasten the cuffs. "You lied about why you were talking to her," she informed him. "If I could, I'd haul your ass to jail for the night for stalking her, but you're lucky Ms. Tappan doesn't want to press charges." She put up the handcuffs, passed over his wallet, and stared at him. "If I hear anything from her about you stalking her again, I will haul your ass to jail."

"Yes, ma'am," Norm answered.

"Now, get the hell off my cruiser and go home."

"Yes, ma'am," he repeated. As Norm started walking to his car, he yanked off the remainder of his tie, which he shoved into his pocket. "That was my best tie," he lamented to the wind.

# chapter four

heri could hear Sophia knocking on the bathroom door with a greater insistence this time. "Come in," Cheri called while finishing plucking her brows. She began brushing her hair as the door opened, revealing Sophia alone. "So, where's Scott?"

"I sent him home," Sophia admitted. "Honestly, he wore me out. So, why are you gettin' gussied up? Got a hot date with Dr. MacPoppinfresh?"

"No," Cheri answered. "Well, at least not that he's aware of, but I've gotta see him."

*I wonder whether I should put on some makeup. Though makeup is a no-no for anyone in preservation, today is my day off, so that rule doesn't apply.*

Sophia chuckled. "You don't need to explain it to me. As dangerous as it might be, you got a taste and you need more. Ambrosia is addictive," Sophia added as Cheri began to line her lips with a pencil, "especially when it's forbidden."

"But he's not my professor," Cheri argued, before grabbing some eyeliner.

"Still," Sophia continued, "if the university finds out, they may have something to say about a PhD student fraternizing with a guest professor."

"Oh, the worst we'll get is a slap on the wrist," Cheri muttered, hoping that would be true.

"Still, you wouldn't want that on your record, would you?" Sophia pulled out some eye shadow and held it out to Cheri.

"Why are you discouraging this?" Cheri looked at her roommate as she grabbed the eye shadow from her and began applying it. "Usually, you'd encourage this behavior."

"Well, I am faculty and you're staff, so we both work for Penton."

"I know it's wrong," Cheri grumbled, "but wouldn't you do him if you were in my shoes?" She set down the eye shadow and picked up some lipstick

"Oh yes," Sophia said without a moment of hesitation. She met Cheri's eyes. "I'd have jumped on him at the coffeeshop, if there had been interest on his part."

Cheri smirked. "You don't have to be so graphic, Sophia, but I'm still going after him." She dabbed some color on her lips, hoping she didn't look extremely pale, as usual. As if she had ever been able to tan and not burn.

"I know," Sophia sighed and then grinned. "I won't say anything. I swear." Her face became serious.

"Thank you." Cheri grinned back at her roommate..

"Good hunting," Sophia called out to Cheri with a wink as she gathered her things and headed for the door.

*And a hunt it will be indeed.*

Cheri finally found an office with a piece of paper taped to the door. As soon as she started to knock, an assistant approached her.

"He's not in right now," the assistant grumbled. "Dr. MacDonough always forgets his meetings. He usually tends to loiter at the museum. Try there."

"Thanks," Cheri said before leaving the hallway. She glanced at her watch and noticed the time: 10:30 AM.

*Damn! I have been searching for an hour and a half!*

She walked to the museum and arrived about fifteen minutes later. Her stomach began to growl, and she wondered whether the coffeeshop at the museum would be open, as chocolate felt necessary. Once she reached the entrance, a security guard grinned at her and waved her through. Since she had been recognized, Cheri began to contemplate the amount of time she spent here. She then meandered through the exhibits looking for Professor MacFi...

*Damn Sophia.*

Her stomach growled again, reminding her that she had skipped breakfast. She decided to get mocha at the coffeeshop and joined the line, when she saw him sitting at the table overlooking the balcony, sipping on coffee. He seemed pensive, lost in thought, though he showed no signs of seeing her.

She now felt torn at the prospect of interrupting him. Cheri glanced away, deciding to go get a sandwich at Javaco and drown her rather irrational fears in something involving lots of chocolate, but when she looked up, Cheri noticed Doctor MacHotstuff staring at her and motioning her to join him.

As she ambled through the crowd towards him, she sniffed the air, smelling the scents from the card last night. Her stomach clenched as she grew nervous, giddy, and a little bit restless

*Okay... I feel quite horny too. If only we weren't interrupted...*

"Hi," she squeaked.

"Good morning, Cheri." His voice wrapped around her like a soft blanket.

She tried to not shiver or grin like a moron.

He smiled warmly at her and asked, "Would you like some mocha?"

She tried to not drown in his eyes. She finally noticed a second cup of coffee next to him. "Is that for me... I mean, of course it is. Thank you. Were you waiting for me?" She then sat down, hoping it would give her a chance to get her brain in gear.

"My TA called and said an insistent young woman was harassing him to get my whereabouts this morning." His smile broadened. "I exaggerate, of course."

She took the mocha and yummed. "How did you know what I was in the mood for?"

As Algernon leaned in to respond, she caught her best view yet of his facial features.

*He has great teeth, but he has a few wrinkles when he smiles and a few silvered hairs. However, those features simply give him more character. Plus, it sorta makes me feel better about the few I have been finding in my hair.*

"It's my true talent," he murmured. "I know instinctively exactly what people want to drink; however, my powers are limited to coffee. I can't do it with wine, beer, or anything else."

"You should moonlight at Javaco," Cheri joked.

"So, did you get anything interesting delivered to you yesterday," he asked, while taking a sip of his drink.

"Why, yes I did. Some crazy stalker that I went out with once stuck a note on my door. I tossed it in the garbage." Cheri winked at him. "No, actually I really like it. The Tarot of Marseilles is one of my favorite decks. At least, it's my guess at first glance. There are several decks based on that one with similar artwork." Cheri took another sip of mocha. "It's the one I use to play with at home. I sorta collect them," she admitted.

"That doesn't surprise me at all. So, you do tarot readings?" His eyes turned impish.

Cheri shrugged. "I'd love to try it, but I actually got them to start a tarrochi playing club. Sophia, that's my roommate, and I," she exhaled, feeling as if she were babbling at this point. "Anyways, she and I have tried to get a big group of friends to play, but it never works out. So, is that card a depiction of yourself or me?" She smirked.

Algernon chuckled. "No, it was partly the idea of the beginning journey the fool represents. Also, it was the first one in the deck outside of the 'how to play tarrochi' instruction card." He leaned in even closer, as if about to share a secret. "Perhaps you'd be interested in seeing the rest of the deck, just to verify it as being the Marseilles deck," he murmured. "It's back in my office."

She could feel her face burn as his eyes delved into hers. "Yes, A..." She looked around the museum and decided it would be better to keep things more professional, "Dr. MacDonough."

*Whew. At least I didn't call him something else, like Doctor Hot-n-Sexy... Damnit, Sophia!*

"Then, lets go," he said. "I believe you already know the way there."

She tried not to cough up her drink as he helped her to her feet.

Cheri sniffed the air a bit as they reached his office corridor, when the same TA from before accosted them.

"I finished arranging the lecture details," the TA panted, looking rather like a dog awaiting a biscuit.

*Do I do the same thing with Dr. Reynolds? Ack! I do!*

"Well done. I have some other preparations that we need for that discussion on Friday afternoon." Algernon passed over a list to the TA, who began reading.

"I guess this will take me the rest of the morning. Call me if there's something else." The TA rushed out, a man on a mission.

Cheri tried to keep from laughing but failed miserably, though she reasoned the TA was well out of earshot and probably didn't hear her. However, her laughter stopped as the office door closed with the click of a lock. She then looked at Dr. MacDonough as he stared down at her. "No cameras," she asked.

"Not one," he replied. Dr. MacDonough…Algernon looked a little tense.

*Perhaps he now has second thoughts about this. Maybe this entire incident is a mistake. But I don't really care. I am going for it!*

She eliminated the distance between them in a few short steps and then murmured, "I don't think we're here to look over tarot decks." She could smell oranges or something citrus-y. At that moment, Sophia's warning from last night popped into her head, and Cheri felt more than a little stupid for musing that over. She gave up and decided, as usual, that she over-thought the entire thing. Her mind made up, Cheri exhaled and then pressed her lips against his.

Algernon embraced her, and their shared kiss became something more visceral and feral. His mouth parted, and their tongues twined. His fingers moved into her hair, and she found herself beginning to kick off her shoes.

Her nipples grew hard under the confines of her clothing. She felt his caresses move to her throat, and she exhaled in anticipation, wanting more. Then she felt his warm hands roam down her back, slide under her skirt, and cup her backside. She wondered whether she wore the nice panties.

*I think I did. I can almost certainly remember pulling on a matching bra and panty set... but what if I really pulled on the one pair of granny panties I ware whenever I just don't want to bother with anything else?*

Her thoughts ceased as he turned and pushed her against the wall, and the engulfing kisses began anew.

Cheri arched against him. She could feel a distinct hardness against her stomach, and she slid a hand over his erection. She thought about the box of condoms tucked away in the bathroom cabinet.

*Damnit, I am so stupid! How could I forget them?*

His fingers brushed over the sides of her panties and slid them down her legs to her ankles.

With a twist, she kicked them off. "I should… uhm…" she began to explain while still rubbing a hand over his loins.

"Ehm?" Algernon's dark eyes turned to her.

"Condom… I forgot…" she whispered.

When he pulled back, she noticed how flushed he appeared to be. He opened a drawer and tossed out a foil wrapper towards her, which she somehow managed to catch mid-air. He moved back to her, and they began again.

Her hands stroked his groin again, and she fumbled to remove his pants. She unfastened his belt, then unbuttoned, unzipped, and pulled down his pants. She then fondled the straining flesh.

She felt him kick clothing aside, and she began to sheath the condom over him.

*If I don't take care of this soon, we will wind up just forgetting the silly thing.*

As he rubbed a hand over her left breast, she felt his thumb trace over the nipple, which throbbed through a bra and shirt. With deft hands, he removed her blouse and bra and then leaned in to whisk his tongue over her swelling breast.

She uttered a strained noise as one of his fingers rubbed her damp entrance and then dipped within her.

*Enough with the foreplay!*

"Inside me now," she panted, as her hand tugged on his phallus.

As his mouth moved back to hers, she found herself against the wall with her hands clinging to his broad shoulders.

Algernon finally filled her with a single thrust, and she began writhing with him. Then she stopped thinking and simply felt.

As Cheri rested against the wall, she considered the past fifteen minutes. She had to look over at Algernon and then back down at her half-naked body to realize it had not been some insane fantasy brought on by hormones. "Wow," she muttered, and then regretted it.

"My sentiments exactly," Algernon panted as he stood up, allowing her a better look at his backside.

*Yup, Sophia couldn't be more right.*

"I could stand to do this again," she admitted.

"So could I," Algernon answered. "Unfortunately, I don't think we have the time."

She sighed. "Why not?"

"I'm assisting with a class in about a quarter of an hour."

"I suppose I should get dressed." Cheri stood up but felt like a fool again, as she was ill-prepared for her conjugal encounter. "I suppose you wouldn't have a napkin, paper towels, or moist towelettes?"

Algernon shifted through his desk again before holding out a selection of moist toiletries to Cheri.

She grabbed a few. As she opened one pouch, she asked, "Are you always this prepared?"

"Only recently." His eyes wrinkled in a smile.

Cheri grinned back at Algernon before beginning to clean herself. "So, since we can't keep on meeting here... can we meet up later at my place?"

"Ehm, it would be sort of uncomfortable with your roommate there." His tone grew serious. "She's faculty, after all."

"Sophia won't say anything," she informed him. As Cheri tossed the used towelettes and their wrappers into the trash can, she wondered for a moment whether this had all been just an elaborate Fick... whatever game for Algernon.

"It's still risky," he said after a brief pause. "Maybe, we can meet up again after this weekend. I'm going to Yale."

"What? Really?"

He smiled again. "Yes. I'm going to talk about the Irish and Roman connection during the Republic era."

She pulled on her panties and started on her bra. "So, you're flying to New Haven?"

"Yes."

"Well, I just happen to be heading there as well. In fact, I have two round-trip, first class tickets."

Algernon pulled up his pants. "So you're going with someone else to Connecticut?"

"No! Well... that is, my parents sent me two tickets so a friend and I could visit them in East Haven, but I'm not going anywhere with that idiot. I planned to return the tickets, but since you're already going," Cheri said before pausing. "How could I say this without sounding like even more of a history nerd? I'd really love to hear your lecture, if you want me to, that is."

While pulling on her blouse, she stared at him, trying to keep her nervousness under wraps.

*If he says 'no', it means that this was a onetime thing, and that would crush me. However, a 'yes' would mean that he might want a relationship. I can't decide which answer worries me more!*

Algernon seemed a little nervous himself, but his eyes put her at ease. "That would be lovely. I was prepared to depart at 10:30 AM tomorrow on Northern, I think."

"Northern? Hmmm. It sounds like we're on the same flight as it is. When you're done with your class, we can head over to the library, and I can put your name on the ticket."

"Thank you. I'm sure we'll have a great time," he said. He walked to the door and unlocked it. He peeked out before picking up her remaining shoe. "All clear, madam librarian," he said.

"I'll be in the third floo–"

He embraced her and kissed her again. "I'll find you." he whispered.

Cheri sat down at the computer and opened up the Northern airline website to check the flight information. Then, she thought it might be useful to clean out her inbox again. She opened her personal email account and grumbled.

*Norm strikes again!*

She blocked his new email, deleted all the messages, and closed her eyes. "Not like this'll do much good," Cheri whispered. She then looked at the clock and wondered whether Algernon would show up. She considered finding his number in the directory, but she realized that she sounded a bit like Norm, at this point. She closed up her email and started to consider reading up on the Yale card collection again, but then she heard a throat clear behind her, and the scent of him wafted in the air. Cheri inhaled and grinned.

Algernon pulled up a chair next to here. "Sorry I'm late."

"No worries," Cheri replied. She relaxed, realizing how tense she had been earlier. She then felt something stiff and plastic touch her thigh. She forced herself not to jump at the unexpected sensation.

"My ID, passport, and so forth," he murmured, before moving his eyes to his own computer screen.

She took the cards and the passport while adapting the air of secrecy. She logged into the airline website again and changed the name on the ticket. When Cheri glanced back at him, she noticed he appeared to be checking soccer, rather football, scores. "I'm done," she whispered, while handing the cards back to him under the desk. She felt like a high-schooler passing notes, at this point.

---

"Thanks. Be sure to pick up the envelope in my chair after I leave," he whispered. Algernon continued looking over the website for a moment, but then he left without a second glance.

Cheri mused for a moment on whether Sophia was wrong.

*Could there be a girlfriend?*

She gritted her teeth and snatched the envelope from the chair.

*I apologize for all the clandestine and furtive encounters between us, Cheri. I just don't want you to get into trouble. I desire to be with you tonight. I feel now that the only way we can meet is at my home. Please meet me here at seven. I'll make dinner. The address is below, my honey.*

*Yours aye,*

*A*

She closed her eyes.

*Maybe I worry too much, as usual.*

Norm watched Cheri stretch a bit as she read the contents of the envelope that the guy had left behind. Earlier, she was looking over and making some adjustments on an airline reservation screen.

He noticed Cheri's skin redden and wondered if it was a love note.

*That's what it is.*

"That's a little nuts for a mousy librarian," Norm whispered to himself and then sighed.

*Then again, maybe she planned on dragging the stranger off to meet her parents instead of me!*

Norm saw Cheri stick the note in her purse and prepare to leave. He lowered his face towards the keyboard and counted to ten, slowly. He exhaled, and turned his head in the direction of the door.

*No Cheri.*

A moment of dread rushed down his spine.

*She is probably waiting behind me. I must get it over with.*

After turning around, he saw no sign of Cheri there either. He then walked out of the lab, trying to see if he could see her.

*There she is!*

He spotted her darting into an elevator, while waving at some of the other librarians there. Norm dashed onto the staircase, arrived at the same floor as she, and followed the group of students wandering through the hallway towards the exit. Cheri darted in and around them with ease.

*Why do I bother? Then again, parental guilt nags at me every time I have*

heather poinsett dunbar & christopher dunbar

*considered dropping the whole thing.*

After leaving the building, he saw Cheri step into her crappy Geo. Norm rushed to his car, jumped in, and started the engine. After backing out, he began trailing her.

*It is a good thing she doesn't seem to be in a hurry, and traffic is fairly light.*

Norm followed Cheri's Geo down a few side streets when he realized she approached the apartment where she lived. Then he witnessed a familiar police cruiser in the distance.

Norm turned into the closest strip center and raced into the first store he found.

"Sign in," a young Vietnamese woman inquired of him while smiling at him from a stool. A blonde woman sat in a massage chair in front of her.

*Crap, I must be in a nail salon.*

"Do you want a manicure, pedicure, waxing," another woman asked while approaching him.

He winced a bit at the thought of waxing. Through the salon's windows, he could see Cheri's car turn into her apartment in the distance.

*At least I can watch her through the window.*

"Pedicure."

*No one would see my feet.*

The second woman grabbed his arm and led him to a chair.

He kicked off his shoes and socks, pulled up his pant legs, and sat down.

Warm water began to fill the tub as the woman turned on the massage chair.

"Excuse me," a voice drawled. He turned and noticed the blonde woman smile at the manicurist in a unique but somewhat familiar accent that Norm could not quite place. "Could you massage my feet for another half hour?"

"Sure, sure, for twenty-five dollars extra," the manicurist replied.

The blonde nodded and said, "Sounds perfect." The young blonde woman then turn her blue eyes toward him, causing him to blush a little despite his attempts to not notice her. "You don't belong here," she observed aloud.

"I'm... sorry?"

"You don't belong here," she repeated. "Sorry, you just don't look the type to be receiving a pedicure. I'm Agnes," she greeted. "Please don't call me Aggie."

"I'm Norman, please call me Norm."

"So, normal guys can get pedicures," Agnes said with a smirk, revealing a sexy twist of a smile. "What brings you to this slice of heaven?"

He considered lying, but he knew he sucked at it. "I think my... uhm ...

girlfriend is cheating on me. She called the cops on me last night, and they're convinced I'm stalking her. So, I started following her home today and was hoping I could ask about this man I saw her with, and well..." He paused and inhaled a breath. "I saw the cops waiting by the apartment and decided to duck in here."

Agnes raised a brow. "Wow, that's either the most creative lie I ever heard and you're nuts or you're telling the truth. If she's not into you, Norm, it's not going to happen."

"She and I were friends for a long time," he explained. "My parents and hers think we should date, but she seems all wrapped up in getting her PhD."

"Hmmm." Agnes stared at her feet. "Sounds like she has the college bug."

"College bug?"

"Yeah, it's my little psychological theory that there are female grad students out there who believe that they're smarter than any woman who goes to college to find husbands and raise a family." Agnes shrugged. "It's why I'm in school."

"Have you had any luck in finding the right man?"

Agnes chuckled. "No, I've just met boys who are only into cars, boozing, and sports. I want someone who can talk about grownup stuff, like getting a house and having kids."

Norm stared at Agnes for a moment. "How old are you?"

*She looks to be in her young twenties.*

"I'm almost 23," she answered.

"I can definitely understand where you're coming from," he told her. "I hope to find a woman like that one day."

"Then, why are you trying to be with this girl who values different things than you?" Agnes stared down at the pink paint on her toes.

Norm sighed. "It's primarily selfish," he admitted. "I don't make a lot of money, and her family has funds to spare."

"Well, money doesn't make happy families, and last I heard, love is free. You probably like this girl, but it doesn't sound like either of you love each other."

"Why do you sound so grown up?"

Agnes shrugged. "I've traveled a lot. It gave me a lot of perspective, I guess. This is great, isn't it?"

Norm stared at Agnes' tan legs. "It's wonderful," he admitted.

## chapter five

As Cheri arrived at the house, she felt a little overwhelmed. It sort of reminded her of the parental units' home in East Haven, as in way too big for a single person to occupy. Cheri noticed an open garage door and witnessed Algernon waving her in. She drove in and parked. She stared at him for a moment, feeling rather confused, but not more so than she had earlier today. As the garage door closed behind him, Cheri noticed a beautiful convertible sitting next to her Geo and felt a little embarrassed.

Algernon opened the driver's side door and offered her a hand. "I apologize for having you park here, but other faculty live on this street."

"I do admit to feeling a little weirded out," she said, giving him a small grin, though her entire body warmed as she took his hand.

*I hope I won't end up sounding like an idiot, again.*

"Still," she continued, "I do appreciate your concern for my reputation. Well, since you're cooking, I brought some red and white wine," she said, before pulling out the bag and passing it to Algernon. "It probably sucks, but–"

"I'm not picky on spirits, and you shouldn't be either," he said, interrupting her. "Thank you." Algernon took the bag. "Did you have any trouble finding the place?"

"None at all."

He took her hand again. "Let me give you a quick tour. You've seen the garage."

"Is that a Morgan," she asked, nodding towards the car.

*Dad has been trying to order one for years.*

"Yes, well, it's sort of a loaner." Algernon blushed a little.

"Someone loaned you… a Morgan," she asked with a raised a brow.

"Yes," he answered, still sounding a little embarrassed.

"You have to take me for a ride in that, later," she suggested.

"To be honest, most of the time I'm afraid to touch that thing. The alarm goes off every once in awhile, and I end up racing out here to find a stupid speck of dust or a fly on it." Algernon nudged open the door to the exterior, and she followed him through a small covered walkway towards the house. Her host pushed through another entrance, and she closed it behind them.

She could hear music playing, smelled something wonderful in the air, and then she heard tags jingling, as a small, white west highland terrier raced towards her and began barking.

"Oh honestly, MacLeod, hush. We just have a guest." Algernon put the wine bottles on a granite counter top.

MacLeod wagged his tail and gave Cheri a plaintive stare and a whine.

"You poor starving boy," Algernon said with a grin. "He has some treats on the counter. Please give him a few, or we'll never hear the end of it."

Cheri found the can of treats. As she grabbed it and opened it, she watched MacLeod's tail began to move faster. She fed him a few treats, and then he retreated to his dog bed, seemingly content and happy.

While noises from kitchen alerted her to Algernon's preparations, Cheri began to examine the house. She observed stone floors, as well as tribal masks, old artwork, and a lot of pictures and paintings lining the walls. She began to study the photographs, scanning them for pictures of her host. While moving off the hard floor onto carpet, she continued to scrutinize the pictures. A few backdrops she recognized. After spotting a picture she remembered seeing before, Cheri leaned in closer to study it, when she felt a hand on her shoulder, making her jump.

"Avebury," Algernon murmured in her ear.

Cheri gave her host a side-long glance and asked, "So you danced around the stones?"

He smiled again. "So did everyone else. It seemed the thing to do." He held out two glasses of wine.

She turned around to face him, took one of the glasses, and raised it to her lips, but Algernon stopped her.

"Ah ah! To your good health." Algernon raised his glass in a toast and then took a few gulps of the wine.

"And to yours. What's that old Irish toast on your cup? Slane chuga?"

He chuckled. "Sláinte chugat, Cheri. So, ever done a crazy dance like that before?"

Cheri took a sip of wine, glanced at the picture of Algernon dancing around a large menhir, and said, "I sorta did something similar in Epping Forest, once. Sort of a crazy dance on a dare from a friend," Cheri admitted. She laughed. "I wound up a muddy mess."

"You lived in London," he asked, taking a few gulps of his wine again. He put down the glass.

"Oh no, Cambridge," she admitted. "I visited London with my roommate, though."

"Oh really, Cambridge," he drawled, before moving in closer. "Want to know something crazy?" He gently wrapped his arms around her.

She put aside her drink, inhaled, and rested her cheek against his chest. "What's that?"

"I thought you might have changed your mind and decided to stand me up." His lips rested against her right ear. "All that talk of dancing..." he paused. "Let's dance now." His voice turned husky.

She tried to keep from making stupid noises. "Alright, but I am rusty," she heard herself say.

"I have a feeling we'll teach each other everything we'd need to know," he purred.

She felt her legs wobble a little and they began swaying together.

"You look so beautiful," he claimed, though Cheri felt otherwise.

She pulled back to stare in his eyes and kissed him, feeling a little stubble rub against her cheek. She felt herself warm at the contact. Cheri forced herself to stop thinking about everything else. In her mind, she pushed her projects aside, her fears, her confusion, and the issues with her family... and Norm. All that remained was the music and Algernon, and some solid object on the floor.

A squeak suddenly brought Cheri out of her reverie, and she lost her balance, landing on her butt in the middle of the floor, grateful she didn't land on the cold stone.

Algernon fell forward next to her, laughing.

MacLeod stood up on her arm, licked her left cheek, and trotted away, apparently pleased with himself.

Algernon turned towards her and slid a hand over her wet cheek, wiping away the slobbery dog-kiss with a warm thumb, before leaning in to kiss her lips. His fingers stroked her cheeks before moving elsewhere, leaving Cheri breathless. His lips opened, and Cheri then attacked him again, tracing her tongue over his, tasting mints over a smoky spiciness. Algernon twined his tongue with hers, intensifying the kiss.

Cheri felt his hands under her shirt, with his thumbs tracing the undersides of her breasts through her bra. She heard herself utter a breathless sound. Cheri reached for Algernon's lap with one hand, while unbuttoning the top buttons of his shirt with her other, finally ripping the rest over his head, impatient with her progress.

He yanked her shirt off and deftly unhooked and pulled off her bra, then he moved his lips to her breasts, with his mouth teasing her nipples as he plumped them.

Cheri used both her hands to undo his belt, enthusiastic and breathless, but then she heard MacLeod whimpering. She looked up and noticed MacLeod from a distance, tilting his head, revealing dog-confusion, and she felt her passion for the moment diminish.

"Algernon," she murmured, before uttering a groan as he nibbled at a nipple. "Algernon, I can't do this while the dog–"

"Ignore him," he hissed, bringing her in for an impatient kiss. Algernon pulled her in closer. As his warm, bare skin came in contact with hers, Cheri felt his erection against the interior of her thigh.

For a moment, she forgot MacLeod, but then the dog's whining began again, and this time Algernon pulled away.

She let out an irritated chuckle at having her passion interrupted again by that dog. Her wetness within burned, and she grumbled a frustrated cry, hoping Algernon would find some way to satisfy her without the dog present.

"Bedroom," he murmured, while tracing a finger over her entrance. He then dipped his wet digit into his mouth while making eye contact with Cheri.

She stood up on shaky feet, protesting in her mind, as his lips encircled the first knuckle on his forefinger. "Tease," she muttered.

"Indeed," he agreed in a guttural whisper. "However, I don't want to be judged by my niece's dog, right now. Plus, I'd rather not have a repeat of carpet burn." He smiled and rose from his seat on the rug.

Cheri looked over him and felt his eyes on her. She felt a moment of embarrassment.

*I am too pale, too short, too plain, too ordinary... and I am... a librarian. He is gorgeous, with great arms, broad shoulders, a nice backside, and a he is a professor! Could I possibly be dowdier?*

Algernon continued staring at her. "What's wrong?" he said as he moved in closer. He leaned in to play with a strand of her hair.

"I'm..." she started to explain, before crossing her arms over her chest and pausing.

"You're stunning" he said.

Cheri stared into his eyes, liking what she heard... even willing to agree, if only to receive the satisfaction she craved.

"Now, will I have to drag you to my bed?" His dark eyes revealed desire and an entreaty.

She felt her face heat. "Take me there."

His hand snaked around hers, and then the stairs seemed to dissolve. Even though she had wanted to examine the rest of the house for hints about him, she found herself in his room, far too quickly to notice anything.

Heat spread through her again, as he placed her hands on his erection. He reached for a drawer next to the bed and grabbed a wrapped condom, which he gave to her. He then sat on the edge of the bed.

Cheri extracted the condom from the wrapper, slid it over his shaft, and then crawled up onto the bed, lying on her back.

Algernon gently mounted her, and their bodies joined again.

She bucked beneath Algernon, thrusting her hips to meet his. Cheri's eyes closed, as the writhing continued. She stopped ruminating over how insecure she felt. He wanted her. Soon her breath caught in her throat, as a clenching spasm overwhelmed her. She moaned into Algernon's shoulder as the pleasure continued and his thrusts moved deeper through her. She became conscious of his calling her name as he began to shudder within her. Cheri closed her eyes, stroking her hands over Algernon as he remained within her.

His heart pounded with hers, and she sighed, content.

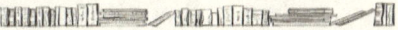

Norm simply stared in awe at the beautiful lawn and grounds of the houses here, as Agnes drove to her home, with him in her car.

She pulled up to one the houses and screeched rubber while turning into a driveway, making Norm's stomach churn. She then turned off the engine.

After opening her car door, Agnes said, "Now, you stay right here and promise not to run away!" Her smile seemed infectious.

He returned her smile. "I promise," he replied.

Agnes giggled, then she darted out of the car and jogged to the large house. While at the front door, she unlocked it and went in.

Norm got out of the car to stretch his legs and started lightly drumming on the roof of her car, considering his luck at meeting Agnes.

*I know she is well-off, but that doesn't even seem to matter, now. She seems perfect and fun. Could I be considering that whole 'love at first sight' shit?*

"That is so clichéd," he muttered. "I just met her, and its just dinner." He fell silent, upon seeing the front door open again.

Agnes stared at him with a somewhat flummoxed look on her face, and he couldn't turn away. As soon as she came back to her car, both of them got in at the same time and donned their seat belts. Then she looked at him and grinned a little.

"So, you found your wallet," Norm asked.

"Yeah," Agnes admitted. "Now I know why my uncle bought a spa package for me."

"Why?"

"Apparently, he has a lady friend with him. At least there was a bra and panties on the floor, as well as some other girly clothing." She chuckled.

Norm raised a brow. "So, what's funny? Ew, you didn't catch them in the act, did you?"

"Nope." Agnes continued laughing. "I'm not really laughing. It's more of a relief thing. My uncle hasn't been with, or hell, even dated anyone since... well... my aunt Elena. She died about five years ago." Agnes suddenly stopped laughing and stared at the garage door. "I mean, she died of cancer, and my uncle just sorta retreated into himself and became a recluse." Suddenly, a small smile reappeared. "So, even if it's just a one-night stand, it's at least stress relief."

She patted his leg, and Norm felt a chill move up his spine.

"So, should I ask about your parents," he asked, stuttering a little.

"Oh my parents live in a castle in Mochrum, Scotland... my dad's auld family place," she drawled a bit.

He realized finally that she had a bit of a brogue.

"They raise sheep," Agnes added. Her smile widened again, making Norm realize she had spoken in jest. "Actually, my mum is a barrister, and my dad is chief surgeon at a hospital." She started the engine and backed out of the driveway. "So, where do you wanna go to dinner?"

*Crap, the infamous question of questions for couples!*

"I'm not sure..." He hoped she knew the town better than he did.

"Okay, then I'll pick." Agnes shifted into drive, and then the two of them were off. A few seconds later, her lips turned up in a sly smile. "So, what about your parents?" Her eyes regarded him for a moment, then returned to the road.

"Oh, they live in a big house with hand-me-down furniture, because they're in debt," he admitted, hearing some disappointment in his voice. "Well, they mean well, I suppose."

"Don't they all," Agnes replied. "So, they probably want you to find someone who can provide well, right?"

"Yeah, that's partly why they're after me to date that girl I was sorta stalking..." Norm sighed. "You sure you wanna go to dinner with me?"

"Yes." Her blue eyes regarded him with calm certainty. "I'm sure by the end of the night, that other girl will be a distant memory."

Cheri and Algernon finally meandered back to the kitchen, though in a somewhat inebriated state. At least she was a little drunk.

Cheri sat down and stared at Algernon, as he stood looking at the stove.

He was dressed in a dark green robe and she had thrown on the button-down shirt he'd been wearing earlier. "Well, at least MacLeod didn't stop in for a snack," he commented. He turned back and snickered a little. "I was going to pull out a chair for you. So, hungry?"

"Sorry to spoil your perfect gentleman record," Cheri said while smiling back at him. "I'm ravenous," she added. "What is for dinner?"

His lips curved into a most enchanting grin. "Mmmmm, first course is a tossed green salad with bleu cheese dressing."

"Oo la la," Cheri purred.

He pulled bowls from the refrigerator and placed one in front of her. "To drink, we have a lovely Alsatian Riesling and spring water." He pulled the bottles out of the refrigerator. He began to pour the wine.

She smiled at him. "So, you're planning to get me a little more tipsy?"

"Oui," he said with a smirk. He then sat down across from her and watched her with glimmering expectation in his dark eyes.

Cheri took a bite of her salad. "This is perfection," she said, after crunching and swallowing. "I may wind up licking the bowl clean."

He chuckled.

"I'm utterly serious," she added, before sipping her wine. "That, or I'll kidnap you and force you to make all my meals for me."

"Mmmmm, maybe I wouldn't mind being kidnapped by you." He sipped at his wine and then took a bite of salad. "So, the next course is pork tenderloin braised in a raspberry chipotle sauce, green beans, and garlic mashed potatoes. Then, we will have crème brûlée for dessert."

"Excuse me while I drool over that." Cheri grinned. "Now, tell me everything about you."

"Everything?"

"Oh yes," she purred.

Their conversation continued through the courses. She learned he had an older sister who was married, who lived in Scotland with her husband, and he had one niece who lived stateside. They discussed politics for a few minutes, then got bored and turned the discussion to art and authors.

As Algernon talked about how his dead wife had written for literary magazines and journals about nineteenth century British authors, Cheri watched his eyes grow sad for a moment, but when then they turned back to her, the sadness faded.

Their topics changed again to organized religion's place in art, then on to spirituality and ghostly encounters.

Algernon looked to Cheri and said, "So, I'm monopolizing the conversation. Tell me about–"

At that moment, her cell phone interrupted them.

"Sorry," she said. "Let's just ignore that. It's probably my stalker." She noticed a strange glint in his eyes, concern, or perhaps even ire. Cheri leaned in and touched his arm. "Don't worry, Algernon. I think he'll get bored and give up. He's just a guy I sorta grew up with, and his parents are pressuring him to chase me. I feel sorry for him, in a strange way. He's nice, but..."

"But?" He touched her fingers, tracing his thumb over her knuckles.

"Meh. He's just the type who wants a woman to follow his lead, have his children, stay at home, and all that. He really needs someone with a strong personality to handle his parents," she admitted. "While he's nice, there's just no... common interests between us. I need someone who can talk about things... like you and I do." She blushed a little and pulled back, playing with her crème brûlée. She felt like a silly student again.

"So, you want an entirely intellectual relationship," Algernon asked while leaning his chin into his hand. His eyes revealed a growing spark of mischief.

"No, I just find intelligence very, uhm... attractive," she answered. Cheri licked her spoon in a seductive a manner, managing to get a rise out of Algernon. "This is really great," she murmured. "In fact, I think I'm still hungry." She stood up, crossed over to him, dropped to her knees, and then opened his robe.

Norm glanced around the tiny restaurant, as Agnes sat down in a creaky booth across from him. The restaurant was pretty much a dive, but it was crowded.

*The food must be good.*

Agnes leaned forward and smiled. "So, you got any quarters," she drawled.

As Norm fished in his pockets, he tried to think over her accent again. Upon finding several quarters, he dropped a few in front of her on the table.

"Thanks," Agnes chirped. She started to flip through songs on the mini jukebox next to the booth. "What are you in the mood for?"

"Seattle garage bands from the nineties," Norm answered without a moment of hesitation.

Agnes giggled a little. "So, where's your plaid and ripped jeans?"

Norm felt his face turn up. "That's a horrible stereotype."

"So you're in disguise," Agnes asked. She put a few quarters in the jukebox, punched a few buttons, and then music started to play. She leaned in closer to him, and he did the same.

After a few moments of his staring into her eyes, Agnes giggled. He found himself laughing a little too. "What is it?" he asked.

"You have dreamy eyes," she purred. Agnes sat up as their waiter, who looked to be about seventeen, came by.

"So what'll it be," the kid asked while looking at Norm.

"I'd like the cheeseburger, fries, and a coke."

"How do you want it cooked?"

Norm raised a brow, impressed.

"Well done," he answered.

"Well done?" Agnes chuckled. "Why don't you ask for a charcoal briquette on a bun?"

Norm smirked. "That's just how I take it."

"Agnes," the waiter asked her while grinning, clearly familiar with her.

"Josh, I'll have the same thing I get every time."

The waiter shook his head. "I shoulda known better."

"Tell Charlie to not shrimp on the sausage, this time," Agnes added.

"I hear you Agnes, but no promises."

Norm looked back at Agnes. "Sausage?"

Agnes motioned him in closer. "I believe hamburgers made with all beef taste like shite. So, I convinced Charlie to mix in one part sausage for every two parts of ground beef for his special customers."

"Special customers?" Norm grinned at her again. He found her attitude to be infectious.

"Charlie thinks he'll get in trouble if he sells them like that to everyone else," Agnes admitted. "So, only a few of us know about it."

Norm looked up and witnessed Josh pouring water for another customer. "Hey… Josh? Could you change mine to a special?"

Josh looked back at him. "I already did. You're sitting with Agnes," he answered.

Norm turned back to Agnes. "So, what plans do you have this weekend?"

Agnes crinkled her nose. "It appears I'm going to Yale."

"Really, Yale?"

"Yeah. My uncle and parents want me to get my masters in psychology at Yale." Agnes shrugged. "It was there or Cambridge."

"So, why go to a dump like Yale?"

Agnes scoffed. "You're one to talk! Where did you get your masters?"

Norm lowered his eyes. "Well, I haven't gotten it yet. I've been working. I'm sure it's a great place. It just sounds boring."

Agnes nodded. "I can understand that. So, you wanna go with me to Yale?"

"Aren't you supposed to be looking over their graduate study program?"

"Well," Agnes drawled a little, "I'm not going there to look over their grad school. That's just what my uncle Al thinks. I'm going there to have fun, but if you have hangups about going places with strange women you just met–"

"Well," Norm mused, "you're about as crazy as I am."

"Flattery will get you everywhere," Agnes replied, before sipping on her water.

"Seriously though, I could be a nutjob," Norm blurted out. "How do you know I'm safe?"

Agnes leaned in. "I'm a good judge of character. I mean, you're stalking this girl, but you misdirect your passions and they're wasted. It doesn't make you crazy… just a little pitiful. Besides, I'm not asking for sex."

Norm tried not to think about that. "Okay, let's go to Yale, but…" he realized there was one problem with the plan. "I don't have a ticket."

Agnes smirked. "I'll see about getting you a ticket, since I invited you," she said, just as Josh arrived to drop off their drinks.

Norm blushed a little as the food arrived. "That's not necessary. I can take care of it."

Agnes patted his hand. "Then, I'll take care of our meals. Too bad Charlie doesn't deliver out there."

Another server dropped off their plates.

"You didn't shrimp on the sausage did you?" Agnes asked.

The stranger smiled at Agnes. "No, I even added extra for you, sweetheart." The unknown server studied Norm. "Josh mentioned you were here with someone that wasn't the uncle. You take good care of her," he advised, while patting Norm on the back, and left them to eat dinner.

Agnes grinned at Norm. "Dig in. I'm sure this'll be worth it."

As Agnes pulled into the driveway and opened the garage door, she saw that a blue Geo rested in her spot.

*Perhaps the visitor remains.*

She unlocked and walked through the sets of doors, when a familiar white bundle of fur raced towards her. Music swelled through the house.

"Hey, sweetiepup," Agnes greeted while picking up MacLeod, trying to avoid his kisses. She noticed kitchen noise and walked into the kitchen, when she spied a woman she didn't know, wearing one of her uncle's shirts and a pair of his boxers, reheating pork tenderloin and green beans. The women turned to face Agnes and her jaw dropped a bit, before she started to button the shirt.

"Hi," Agnes chirped. She was in a great mood, even though Norm tempted her past the 'no second base on the first date' rule. "You're my savior, right?

The one banging my uncle Al?" Agnes moved past the other woman and opened the refrigerator while still holding MacLeod, who tried to grab some of the leftovers. She put him down on the floor before taking two bottles of water and some grapes. She then noticed that uncle Al's date still looked to be in shock. "I'm sorry, I didn't mean to startle you," Agnes began. "I'm Agnes. Want some water?"

"Uh, thanks," the other woman said after finding her voice. "I'm Cheri… Tappan." Cheri rubbed her hand on a towel and took the extended water bottle. She opened it and took a sip before placing the after-dinner snack on a plate.

Agnes sat at the dinette table, followed by Cheri.

"So, I'm your savior?" Cheri asked.

Agnes nodded her head. "My poor uncle hasn't had a date, much less a decent lay, in five years. He's sweet, but intense and just plain… tense," Agnes stated, sipping her water.

Cheri grabbed her fork and cut into the tenderloin. "I like his intensity," she admitted.

Agnes watched Cheri smile and turn pink. "Probably you and he are a lot alike," Agnes said. "So, what do you do for a living?"

"I'm working on my doctorate in preservation and special collections of rare books," Cheri answered, with the utter delight of a person who wanted to spend the rest of her life at a university.

*Uncle Al usually says the same sort of thing whenever someone asks.*

Agnes grinned. "Wow… so where do you work?"

"I'm a glorified librarian," Cheri replied.

"Oh, that sounds sorta… interesting."

*At least Uncle Al would find it interesting.*

"I love it," Cheri exclaimed with a grin, before eating some green beans. "So, what are you studying?"

"I'm a senior psychology student," Agnes admitted. "However, I have no desire to make a career of it." She began popping the grapes into her mouth.

"Really? Why not?" Cheri appeared to be concerned. She speared another piece of pork and began chewing.

"Oh, I just wanted to learn how to manipulate a husband and any future spawn we might have."

Cheri burst out laughing and coughing.

"Easy girl, don't choke! Take sensible bites," Agnes said, noting her words made the other woman laugh harder.

Cheri sipped on her water again and regained control. "Why not take your education to the next level," she asked.

"Well, I was at the museum... when you yelled at your date." Agnes smirked. "I definitely can respect and appreciate your opinion, but I'd feel fulfilled by raising children and taking care of a man. Last I checked, graduate level education is not a requirement for that job, at least until the kids become teenagers." She smirked again. "Then, all bets are off."

Cheri chuckled again. "You might be selling yourself short, but I can appreciate that you know what you want from life, and you're on the way there. You are on the way there, right?"

"Mmmmm." Agnes grinned. "I met a great guy today. He's everything I'm looking for–"

"Agnes," Uncle Al called out in surprise while staring at her, obviously oblivious she was home, owing to the loose robe he work, which he tried desperately to tighten with a great deal of nonchalance, drawing laughter from both women in the room.

Agnes snorted a bit. "I said I'd be back around eleven, and it's a quarter to twelve."

Her uncle uttered a strained chuckle. "I guess I lost track of time."

Agnes finished up the grapes. "So, did you have a good night?"

"Uh huh," he muttered, while starting to turn red.

Agnes smirked. "He must really like you, Cheri. He's blushing! That's so adorable."

"Well," he said, before clearing his throat, "we need to get up early so we can go to the airport." He sat down next to Cheri.

Agnes then caught her uncle casually tracing a finger over Cheri's bare thigh, seemingly hoping the movement was unnoticed, which it wasn't.

"Uncle Al!" Agnes attempted to sound stern. "You lack authority without your trewes, and I'm already packed. I think I'll leave you two on your own, now." She smirked and stood up.

"Oh, Agnes, it turns out we have an extra ticket for New Haven," her uncle said. "Cheri has an extra first class ticket, and she invited me to fly with her."

"Oh, I see." Agnes smirked. "Very well. I suppose I can try to find someone to join me in coach. Nice meeting you, Cheri. Thank you again." She patted her uncle's shoulder while passing him and whistled for MacLeod to follow her. She pulled then out her cell phone and searched for Norm's number. She called it as she began to trot up the back stairs.

"Wha????"

"Hello, sleepyhead," she purred to Norm. "So, I've got some good news. I have a plane ticket for you. All you need to do is pick me up at around eight AM."

# chapter six

lgernon awoke upon hearing the piercing cadence of his alarm, and he grumbled, before pulling the pillow over his head. He allowed the alarm to grow louder as he mused over the activities of the last night.

*It seems like an old dream, and the simple reality now is that I am alone... and being lonely sucks!*

"Would you turn that damn thing off already? I'm awake, now," a woman's voice groaned, probing past the pillow and the alarm.

*She sounds cranky. Elena always hated–*

When an arm wrapped around him, he broke from his dream-state to remember Cheri had spent the night, that he was not alone. He smiled, willing himself to forget that he first thought Elena slept next to him.

"Algernon," Cheri muttered, patting his chest.

"Okay," he grumbled, while uncovering his face. He felt a strange mixture of relief and pleasure. He reached over and hit the alarm button, before rolling around to face her, trying to forget his earlier assumption. He rubbed his eyes and stared across at Cheri.

She blinked and returned his stare. "Are you alright," she asked.

"I'm fine," he replied. "We better get ready to go." He traced a finger over the strands of her hair.

Cheri sat up. "I call toilet," she cried out before racing out of the bed and into the bathroom.

As he watched her fleeting, naked form, he noticed the tattoo on her lower back again. He suddenly felt ancient. At that moment, he heard the door to the loo close. Algernon lay back in bed and closed his eyes for a minute or two. After stretching a bit, he sat up and grabbed his pajama bottoms. He pulled them on, wandered into the bathroom, and sat down on the rolling vanity chair, staring at himself in the mirror.

*When did all the gray hairs show up?*

"What are you thinking? What could you possibly offer her? You're damaged goods. You'll never have that level of comfort with her," he informed himself in a half-whisper.

*I should tell Cheri to go home and find a real man that could handle a relationship.*

The flush of the loo broke Algernon from his musing, and he watched with astonishment as Cheri opened the door to the water closet and bound over to him.

*She has gone from cranky to quite pleased in a very short time.*

She leaned in and embraced him while he watched her through the vanity mirror. "Well, don't you look sexy in your pj's," she purred. Cheri kissed his cheek and then sauntered back into the bedroom. She returned with a makeup bag and started to brush her teeth.

He decided to wait until she finished dressing before suggesting she go home.

Cheri turned towards him, instead of his mirror image, after spitting into the sink. She wiped her lips. "You look miserable," she commented. Her youth faded as she continued to look worried.

Algernon shrugged. "I do? I suppose I'm a little stressed with the idea of my upcoming lecture."

*That wasn't really a lie. My colleagues may laugh at my findings. What if all the exhibits never arrived?*

Cheri smiled. "I know how to relieve stress," she drawled, before spinning his vanity chair so he faced her. She then dropped to her knees on the carpet, unbuttoned his pyjama bottoms, and pulled out his now erect penis.

Algernon closed his eyes as she began to lick and suckle its head.

*Elena said life should be lived. Life involved love, and she informed me once she'd haunt me if I didn't stop moping after she passed.*

Algernon stroked Cheri's hair and head with both hands. He found her to be somewhat similar to Elena. They shared the same attractive traits, yet Cheri seemed more playful, at times.

Algernon stopped thinking, realizing it felt wonderful to be desired.

Cheri looked up at Algernon, wiped her mouth, and asked, "Do you feel better, now?"

"Yes," Algernon said, while tracing a finger and thumb over her cheekbone, causing her to smile. "Much better, thank you."

He leaned in to kiss her, but Cheri held up her hand, assuming he would prefer her to brush her teeth again first. She stood up to do exactly that, when she caught sight of the alarm clock in the bathroom mirror. "I'd love you to reciprocate, but it looks like we don't have much time." She stood and began to wash her face and prepare her toothbrush again.

"Mmmmm," he murmured while standing up and wrapped his arms around her. "Perhaps on the plane." He kissed her left shoulder before moving to the second sink.

"You are so naughty," she drawled as she washed off her face. However, when she noticed Algernon pick up a razor, she walked over to him and pressed her breasts against his back. Cheri stroked his bristly cheeks with both hands. "You'd look so handsome with a beard," she uttered in a half-sigh.

"I haven't had a beard since–"

Cheri spun him in the vanity chair to face her and kissed him.

He put down the razor and smiled. "Alright then. I will keep the beard. For you."

Cheri kissed his forehead and then walked back to the right vanity. She began to dress.

Algernon continued his grooming regimen. As he applied his deodorant, he watched her pulling on a tee, concealing her lovely breasts.

She caught him watching her. "Yes?" She grinned as she pulled her hair away from her face.

"You're so good to me."

She chuckled. Cheri then grabbed the rolling vanity chair and sat. She looked pointedly at him and said, "You realize we don't have time for any further fun activities, don't you?"

"No," he answered, while glancing over at the sink and then at her through the mirror. As he watched her reflected image, he could see her eyes regard him with a sparkle. "I mean, you just know how to read me and take care of me." Algernon scooted his vanity chair closer to her.

"Well, you're easy to read," she admitted. "Aren't you going to get dressed?"

With their knees now touching, he sat up and kissed her, before pulling her off the vanity chair. He then lifted her onto the vanity and spread her shapely legs apart.

*I'm glad she hasn't donned her knickers, yet. So much for arriving early at the airport.*

Agnes felt her consciousness ripped from her dreams upon hearing a violent knock on the door. She groaned, "What?!"

"Agnes? We're about ready to leave. The cab is here," she heard her uncle say. "Are you ready to go?"

*He never takes my churlish morning attitude to heart, simply because he also needs tea or coffee to wake up.*

"Still sleeping," Agnes growled. "A friend will pick me up." She heard some noise from MacLeod and realized that she and Norm would need to drop him off at the minder's.

"I'm glad the ticket won't be wasted," he said through the closed door. "I guess we'll see you at the airport."

"Aye," she muttered. She soon heard the sound of a doorbell and voices. A moment later, she heard the door close, and then Agnes stared at the clock.

*Great. Five minutes till the alarm.*

Agnes closed her eyes and rubbed her nose, hoping she could sleep more. Then she thought of the trip and spending time with Norm, which excited her, compelling her to get out of bed and start her morning. As she slid her feet out from onto the floor, the covers moved. Agnes lifted a corner, revealing MacLeod staring up at her, bleary-eyed. After petting him, she reached over and switched off the alarm.

*Everything awaits downstairs. Now, I just need to pack up MacLeod and get dressed.*

Agnes considered eating a bowl of cereal but then looked at the clock. Instead of cereal, she grabbed a granola bar. At that moment, she heard the doorbell ring. She rushed to the door, flung it open, and jumped into Norm's arms, kissing him. "We have a short detour, but let's get going," she said before passing him a suitcase. She then grabbed MacLeod's carrier, grunting at the dog's weight.

Cheri hiccupped as the plane taxied to the terminal at the New Haven airport. She then looked up at the seat belt sign, wondering when it would go off.

*Bing*

As soon as the chime sounded, the first class passengers, including Cheri, rose in a rush to get out. Cheri leaned against her chair as she stood up, feeling the tug from the champagne remaining.

*Why did I agree to a second glass? Algernon manages to look rested, yet awake, after three single malt scotches, neat no less!*

She wobbled a bit, while grabbing her purse and carry-on, grateful Algernon stood behind her blocking the other first class passengers, allowing her to squeeze out. She strode out of the plane and through the walkway, only slowing down to allow Algernon to catch up.

"Looks like you need some water," he commented.

"I've apparently become a lightweight," she replied. "Believe it or not, I had tolerance, once. Apparently, it disappeared when I started grad school."

Algernon pulled away her carry-on. "Nothing wrong with being a cheap drunk." He smirked at her.

Cheri giggled while covering her mouth. "I assume we need to pick up the luggage downstairs."

Algernon wrapped an arm around her and led her to an elevator to baggage claim.

"I need to… powder my nose," she said as they approached the claim area.

*Somehow, loudly stating that I have to use the loo seems a bit inappropriate.*

"I will keep an eye out for your suitcases," he said.

After leaving her belongings with Algernon, she weaved through other passengers to the bathroom. Once there, she got to the sink and splashed water on her face. While staring at herself in the mirror, she contemplated her current state and how she could recover.

*After we get the luggage, I can nap in cab and at the hotel. Stupid champagne!*

Cheri wiped her face and stepped out of the bathroom. After weaving through the crowd of travelers, she approached Algernon, who noticed her arrival.

"Well, Agnes apparently got out of bed and found her way to the plane."

"I'm glad to hear that," Cheri said with a chuckle.

"Yes. I met her friend, too." Algernon smirked.

"Oh? Yes, she mentioned him last night. Does the mystery guy have a name?"

Algernon grabbed a suitcase. "I believe he said his name was Norm."

Cheri started to cough.

*No, it has to be a crazy coincidence.*

Algernon continued without seeming to notice Cheri's discomfort. "Interesting guy, well… not really." He grinned. "But, he seems safe, and he's polite, at least."

Cheri soon noticed Agnes, with her hair pulled back into a ponytail.

*Damn…is she ever not cute?*

Agnes managed to grab a huge suitcase and pass it over to another blonde–

*Norm? My Norm? Well, not mine, but definitely the one I know.*

"I gotta use the loo again," she practically shouted, causing several people to look her way, apparently shocked at the outburst.

Algernon turned back to her. "Are you sick?" His dark eyes now revealed concern.

"Fine, I'm fine. I just drank too much, and… I'll meet you at the cabs!"

He wrapped his arms around her waist.

She almost wanted to melt into those arms.

"We have a car coming to pick us up, remember," he reminded her.

"Okay, that's right! I won't be long!" She laughed, before racing back to the bathroom. Cheri sat down in a stall and closed her eyes. "Calm down," she ordered herself in a strange mantra. "Everything will be fine."

"Honey, are you okay," a woman called out from another stall.

"Yes, I'm good," Cheri answered. "I'm just having a small nervous breakdown," she muttered. She willed herself to count to ten… or more.

As Agnes gathered her bags, Norm took a moment to stare at her hips and backside and then chided himself for doing so. He then straightened his luggage, preparing to leave once she retrieved her remaining suitcase.

"Norm?"

Norm looked behind him and noticed Mr. and Mrs. Tappan walking towards him.

"Hello, sweetie," Mrs. Tappan greeted before embracing him for a moment.

Norm glanced around while Mr. Tappan shook his hand, realizing he had forgotten they would be here and that his parents would be with them.

*Not to mention they would expect Cheri here too.*

"So, how are you doing," he asked, trying to think over how to approach this subject. The chorus of fines did little to reassure him of an escape plan

"So, where's my pumpkin?" Mrs. Tappan chuckled. "Let me guess, bathroom?"

Norm grinned and tried to think of what else to say. "I need to be honest," he began. "I apologize for not calling earlier, but Cheri isn't with me today. In fact, she and I went on one disastrous date, and that was it." He watched her parents' faces fall to disappointment.

"We all thought they were…," Mr. Tappan said, before looking over at his wife. "Did I miss something?"

"She didn't call to cancel her flight." Mrs. Tappan's frown turned to anger. "Oh, that brat!"

Norm sighed. "I'm not sure why she didn't call," he admitted, feeling some relief that it wasn't his fault and that he didn't have to try to impress them. "Anyways, I'm here with another friend, and it looks like we're ready to go, so I guess you should give her a call. Tell her 'hi' for me." He grinned. "As far as I know, she's still in Ohio. Nice to see you two again. Tell my parents, when you see them, that I'll call them later." Norm then turned on his heel and headed towards Agnes.

"So, who's that?" Agnes asked.

Norm leaned in for a kiss as he took her carry-on. "Some friends of my parents. I don't really like them. Let's go." He started rolling their luggage towards the cabs.

Cheri got the nerve to peek out of the bathroom and watched her parents talk to Norm, before ducking back into the bathroom. She heard noise as other flights were announced and more baggage began to move through the concourse.

*Perhaps now would be a good time to try to escape.*

She ducked behind a large family and their suitcases and stopped behind a wide column. After glancing around the column, she started moving with a group of drivers picking up people and moved through the exit. She found Algernon standing in front of a town car. She opened the back passenger door, jumped into the car, and scooted to the opposite side.

Algernon gave her a confused stare before climbing in after her. "Are you in a hurry," he asked.

Cheri leaned in closer. "There was a long line, and the stalls were vile," she said. She hated lying, but being caught by her parents at this point seemed much worse. Cheri crossed her legs.

"I see," Algernon replied. "Can you hold it until the hotel?"

Cheri nodded her head.

Algernon turned back towards the driver. "Please go as quickly as is reasonable."

"Yes sir."

Cheri squirmed in her seat, now needing to actually go. As they drove away, she spied Agnes and Norm climbing into a cab behind them, as well as her parents leaving the airport, looking pissed. Cheri slid down in her seat.

Algernon turned back to her. "What's wrong?" He tucked a strand of her hair behind her ear.

"I'm still feeling the effects of the champagne," Cheri lied. She could see the cab carrying Agnes and Norm still following them. She then realized at that point that they were staying in the same hotel.

*Crap! Can't I ever escape Norm?*

"It's great to be here, again," Algernon announced, while turning to look at the sights surrounding them.

"Yes, it's beautiful," Cheri admitted, feeling stupid again. Wishing to distract herself, Cheri looked through the front windshield at the traffic ahead of them. She then noticed the traffic light ahead of them turn yellow. She hoped Norm and Agnes' cab would stop.

*Please, please, stop.*

She inhaled in relief as the cab behind them stopped at the light.

*Thank God for small mercies.*

Soon, the hotel loomed in the distance.

Cheri inhaled and relaxed. "I'm happy to be here," she said to Algernon. "Thank you." She leaned in and kissed him.

He smiled back at her, his eyes revealing some unknown secret. "You're welcome."

Once the town car pulled up to the hotel entrance, Cheri stepped out without waiting for the driver. "Call me when you get to our room, please," she said to Algernon. "I'm sure the bathroom here will be much better."

"Alright," Algernon acknowledged as he stepped out of the car. He pulled her in for a kiss. "Don't take too long. I have something planned for us."

Cheri heard herself utter a strained giggle as she casually strolled through the doors. However, when she saw Norm's cab turned a corner, she started to rush for a hideaway. While looking for the bathroom, she found the bar and decided it would be a good place to hide for a little while, once she finished her business.

As Algernon stepped into the lift with the porter, he picked up his cell phone again.

*I hope this won't put a damper on the afternoon activities I've planned.*

"Hey! Hold please," he heard Agnes shout.

He pushed the hold button, and Agnes and Norm raced in. "How is it that you two get the nice room and I get the bargain," he asked Agnes.

"Because, you let me make the reservation for me, and the university handled yours," Agnes answered with a smirk.

"So, now we all realize that you can't be trusted?"

"No, it means that I'm better at getting good deals than the university," Agnes chided.

As soon as the door opened on their floor, he and the porter began to exit the elevator. "So what are your dinner plans," Algernon called out to them.

"Room service," Agnes replied, before the door closed.

Algernon chuckled and then followed the porter toward the room.

Norm followed Agnes into their room. "So, what did you mean by room service," he asked Agnes.

Agnes dumped her luggage on the floor. "Oh, that was just to get Uncle Al out with his date. Otherwise, we'd have to listen to him and her talk about boring intellectual stuff all night."

"So, what do you wanna do," Norm asked, though he knew what he wanted to do.

"I wanna have fun," Agnes said with a wide grin. "Don't you?"

---

heather poinsett dunbar & christopher dunbar

"Sure!"

*Finally... action!*

"Okay," Agnes said, before grabbing her purse. "Let's go."

"Go?"

"Yeah, I've got a list of places where we can have fun," Agnes replied.

As Agnes studied him, and Norm realized she deserved better than being just more than the role he assumed she would take. "Alright, then. Let's go."

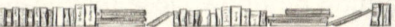

Cheri sipped at the lukewarm water, grateful that the bartender suggested it would be best to get rehydrated instead of getting tipsy all over again, while old 80's new wave played in the background. She felt things were starting to make sense again, when her cell phone beeped. She pulled it out of her purse, but then Cheri realized the ring came from another person's phone, as hers remained off. She felt stupid, realizing that she had forgotten to turn it back on. Cheri turned on the phone and watched it connect to the network, only to see fifteen messages appear on the screen. "Holy crap," she muttered. She started playing the voicemail messages.

*"Hey pumpkin, its mom. We're leaving to meet you and Norm at the airport–"*

Cheri deleted the rest of the message, fearing the worst. The cell phone moved on to the next voicemail... her mother, again.

*"We're here! Waiting–"*

Cheri hit the keypad, and the phone moved on to the next message.

*"We've checked the bathrooms–"*

Cheri deleted the message again.

*"Where the hell are you? Why haven't you called?"*

She deleted again.

*"Your father is furious. He wants to disown you. At the very least, you need to pay us back for the wasted airfare."*

The next eight messages seemed to be along the same tangent. Cheri glanced around, hoping not too many people were hearing this. She paused, wondering why she bothered with this, but decided to risk listening to the rest of the messages. The next one was from her father.

*"Cheri, I'm sorry for what we said. Don't worry about the airfare. Just call us. We get the point."*

She saved that message and moved on to the next, which was from Algernon, who sounded almost as worried as her parents.

*"Cheri? Where are you? You aren't sick are you? I'll meet you in the lobby. We have to leave soon to get to the surprise."*

Cheri closed the phone and stood up. She paid her bill and started for the lobby. She decided to call her parents on the way.

"There you are! Let's go," Algernon said upon seeing her. He then stood and took her elbow. "I've got a cab waiting."

Cheri hung up her cell phone without calling them.

"So, where are we going?" She chuckled with nervous anticipation. His smile proved infectious.

"No guessing," he insisted. "It's a surprise, my honey."

She considered warning him how close they were to her parental units, but then he started talking again... and she found herself lost, listening to Algernon speak. While he spoke, she had a strange mental image of Algernon at his place, in the buff, reading the classifieds to her.

"*For sale, lawn mower. Engine missing. Fifty dollars or best offer. Motivated seller.*"

She blinked away the image and wondered whether she'd ever get past his voice. She soon shifted her mind back into her reality and smiled at him. "Tell me again how you found the artifacts in Bath?"

"I was exploring the caved-in area beneath the floors under the museum. There were so many basements and hidden rooms and vaults. Anyway, after I went to the lower levels, the rope fell, and I was stuck inside for a few hours. While there, I found some unexplored vaults and rooms."

"I'd love to see that," Cheri admitted.

"Well, it is closed to the public, but seeing that you know the lead archeologist, I think I can sneak you in," he purred.

She studied the beautiful landscaping as they pulled up to the museum on campus. "This is the perfect date, you know." She chuckled, giddily.

"Your surprise awaits us," he drawled, while opening the door. He took her hand.

"I can't wait!"

# chapter seven

Agnes felt Norm had been a gentleman so far, and he had been gentle. Granted, he could be a little soft, but not too soft. He didn't spend too much time on intellectual pursuits. After all, the rest of her family lived for that. He didn't even mention *her*.... the other girl, woman, whatever, faded into the distance. Part of her wondered what was that nut job's problem.

*Why wouldn't anyone want someone like Norm? Oh well, the girl in question has to be the biggest git on the planet earth. The unknown girl's loss could be my gain.*

Agnes looked over at Norm and smiled, trying to keep her naughty thoughts at bay. She watched him study the scenery from the cab window, before placing a hand on Norm's right thigh.

He turned towards her and smiled. "Yes?"

"Oh, nothing," she admitted, returning his smile. "I just wanted to touch you. Is that okay?"

"Of course," he drawled. He shifted his weight so her hand could shift ever so slightly towards his crotch.

She teased him again to see how far she could push him before they reached Ingalls Rink. Norm seemed to trust her enough to not ask where they were going. She knew they would stop soon. She leaned in to kiss him.

Norm leaned in too and started to close his eyes, but at that moment, the cab came to a sudden stop and then parked. Norm pulled back. "How much," he asked the driver.

"Let me take care of this," she told Norm.

"Okay," he said, grinning. He stepped out of the cab and waited to assist her. As he waited, she could see him looking around at the building. "You're taking me to a Yale hockey game?" His eyes lit up.

"Aye," she replied with a relaxed shrug. She liked hockey, well, more than any other American sport.

"I love you," Norm admitted. He shook his head, looking over the rink.

"Well, I love you too," she answered in a quiet tone.

"How did you know that I liked hockey," he asked, while meeting her eyes again.

"You talked about it at the nail salon," she commented.

"You listened?"

"Of course I listened! I like talking to you. So, let's go. There are more surprises."

"I can't wait!" Norm grinned as they approached the front gate.

While they walked, Agnes handed over the tickets and smiled.

A few minutes later, once they went through the usual bag and purse inspections, an usher led them to seats directly behind the glass and near the penalty box.

"I think I'm gonna faint," Norm said. He chuckled. "I'm not afraid to admit that."

"Don't you dare faint! You'll miss the good stuff," she informed him.

He looked like a child at Christmas.

After Agnes sat down next to Norm, she felt his arm around her, and she pressed herself in closer to cuddle with him.

"Did I tell you that I loved you," he asked.

Agnes nuzzled his face with her lips. "Yes, you did. I love you too." She then kissed him on the lips.

*Damn boxers. Stupid, stupid boxers.*

Algernon decided it would be best to start thinking of a statistics class he had taken many, many years ago. "What was I thinking," he muttered, as his mind wandered away from statistics and back towards her.

*Cheri may probably wind up being so excited that they end up in a closet together. It could be possible. Alright, that was more than a little unlikely.*

Cheri turned towards him. "What are you thinking," she asked.

He tried to keep his thoughts of her reactions to his surprises at bay. "Oh, nothing important," he lied, deciding to think about statistics again, as he took her hand to lead her to the basement, where the security guards scanned his credentials again and examined Cheri's drivers' license and educational IDs.

"I've never been in this section before," Cheri whispered. She revealed a somewhat nervous smile. "I love this museum and the campus library."

"Why don't you work here," he asked. "After your PhD," he added.

"Maybe..." she muttered, before sliding her ID back into her wallet. "Then again, I like some distance from my parental un..." Cheri sighed. "They're nice, but–"

"They're a bit obsessive when it comes to their only child," he reasoned aloud.

"Mildly," Cheri admitted. "Yeah and uhm... they invited me to some dinner party tonight. I guess I'll run by and…" She began to look uncomfortable. "Anyways," she added, seemingly to push aside the topic, "what's down here? Zombies? An ancient Native burial ground? A secret vampire lair?"

Algernon laughed. "Not quite. You'll see. Don't worry, we're allowed here."

"It's just with so much security guards here, I'm thinking that I'm in the White House."

"You'll see." He approached a door hidden by shadows and began to knock.

George opened the door and peered at him for a moment before pulling out a pair of glasses.

"Algernon? I… is it already two?" George looked over his watch. "Damn… lost track of time, again."

"Two and a quarter, according to the clock on the opposite wall," Algernon replied.

George put on his glasses and grinned. "Nice to see you again. It takes awhile for me to adjust to these. Stupid eye surgery never worked."

"Nice to be seen," Algernon replied. "It's nice to see you as well. You will be here for the lecture, right," he asked, while glancing back at Cheri.

"Wouldn't miss it," George replied. "So, is this your friend with the interest in–"

"Ah," Algernon interrupted him. "Let's keep the mystery going for a bit. Cheri, this is an old friend, Dr. George Travers. George, Cheri Tappan."

George grinned. "The Cheri Tappan who wrote the paper on new greener methods for the preservation of tarot collections?"

"One and the same," Algernon answered, though he quickly saw Cheri's jaw slacken in shock.

*George can't be depended upon for keeping secrets. I should have known better. Oh well. This will still prove to be worthwhile.*

"I'm flattered…," she stuttered. "I didn't think anyone had read that."

"I'm someone," Algernon admitted.

"You read it too," Cheri asked while turning back to him.

"In the last few days," he answered. "I found it in the electronic databases at work."

"Dr. Reynolds sent it to me," Dr. Travers replied. "It's intriguing. I'm not so certain about the methods you espouse, but I know I'm tired of coughing and sneezing from possible exposure to somewhat out-dated chemicals. So, are you ready to see this surprise?"

Cheri grinned. "Is this what I think this is?"

"It's in our private lab," George added. "Come, follow me."

George held the door open, and Cheri walked through, with Algernon following them both, to a secured door with a card reader and sensor. George swiped his card and placed his thumb on the sensor, causing the door to buzz. With the door unlocked, George opened the door and led the party into the dark and cold interior.

Algernon could barely see beyond the floor, but he could distinctly hear the exit door close and latch behind him.

*Click*Click*Click*

Then the lights turned on.

Cheri and George quickly donned gloves and masks set out on top of a credenza near the door.

Algernon also grabbed a pair of gloves and a mask, even though he figured he wouldn't be touching the display.

Cheri covered her head with a hair cover, and they headed to another area.

The group passed by rows of cabinets towards a table holding several boxes, some opened and some still under lock and key. A lighted armature and magnifying glass hung from the ceiling, while camera equipment rested on another table with a laptop.

Cheri approached the table and inhaled. "Ohmygod," she whispered. "The Cary-Yale Visconti deck?"

George nodded. "The oldest deck in existence."

"I've wanted to see this since I started my undergrad in history." Cheri's voice choked.

"Well, since you have handled rare collections, you know the rules. Have a seat, and let me know if you'd like to have any pictures.

Cheri sat slowly, as if afraid to go faster. She stared at the cards for a moment.

Algernon moved in a little closer to observe her. He saw her forehead turn pink and her eyes dilate, but after a moment of excitement, Cheri seemed to take control of her emotions. He looked on as she pulled out the tools and began to carefully examine the Fool. Algernon hoped the next exhibit would be as exciting for her as this one appeared to be.

*Who am I kidding? She'll be thrilled.*

Cheri wondered whether she might be drooling, though she reasoned that at least the mask would hide anything embarrassing. She then tried to gain access to her mind. "Pictures," she muttered, while turning to Dr. Travers. "Can I take pictures of the major arcana?"

He smiled. "Of course you can. Do you need help setting up? Though,

I'm certain you've done this before–"

"Penton doesn't have this kind of equipment," Cheri answered. "I have no idea how this will work," she admitted.

"Not a problem, then." Dr. Travers sat down in a rolling chair and glided over to the computer. "Pull down that camera... there you go." He began to study the image of the card on the computer screen.

She looked back at Algernon for a moment.

*How can I possibly ever thank him?*

After a few hours watching Cheri carefully study and take pictures of the Visconti deck, Algernon strolled through the familiar hallways through the rest of the artifacts while trying to wrap his mind around what these findings would really mean.

*Why would a Republic era Roman name show up during Charlemagne's era? I have ignored these elements, and I plan to let others figure the meaning and mysteries. However, the ensuing controversy should be hard to ignore.*

While deep in thought, he looked at Cheri, who had seemed reluctant to leave the tarot collections in the card and game museum behind at first. However, her eyes now studied the exhibits surrounding them. He then noticed Dr. Walker approaching them, so Algernon extended his hand.

After the two shook hands, the curator stared at Cheri for a moment and smiled big. "Welcome, welcome," he began. "I see you brought a guest to look over the exhibit before we open it to the public."

"Yes, this is Cheri Tappan. Cheri, this is Dr. Winston Walker, the curator."

Cheri smiled and nodded to Winston.

"Cheri and I were looking at the Card and Game Museum earlier, and I wanted to show her this exhibit, too," Algernon answered, wishing the curator would stop staring at Cheri. "So, where is it," he asked, while rubbing his hands together.

"It's in our most secure wing," Walker replied before smiling. "Do prepare yourself. Only a few individuals in our community have seen this." Winston turned and motioned for them to follow him to another security desk with a log. "I assume you know about how this collection was found," Walker said to Cheri.

Cheri nodded her head as she signed the log. "Under what had been a Roman villa in Bath, England," she answered. "Algernon told me all about it. Can we start our tour, now?"

Winston met Algernon's eyes, revealing disappointment that Algernon had stolen his thunder, so to speak. "Alright, let's go to the first room." He lead the party into the room on the right, which Algernon knew was the Coin

---

and Jewelry Collection. Coins and jewelry decorated display cases, while a timeline listed the eras of coins discovered, and a few mosaics lined the walls. "Some of these coins go back to before the invasion of Britannia," Walker said, before looking back at Algernon. "Right?"

Algernon nodded his head. "Yes, there are coins here from every Roman era, as well as other eras and regions of the world. For example, we found Frankish livres with Charlemagne's picture, and the jewelry..." he sighed.

"Exquisite," Cheri whispered. "I love the torcs and bracers. I mean, here we have the Roman key patterns and Celtic knotwork intertwined again." She stared at a necklace for a moment. "Is this Chinese?"

"Yes, that's one of the oddities of the vaults," Algernon added. "Did you see that unpolished diamond in the back of the display?"

"Is that what that is?"

"Yes, I suppose they may have traded for it..." Algernon shrugged. "It looks like these people traded with Africans, Chinese, Frankish, Indians, Persians, the Romans..." His voice trailed off again. He then looked at Cheri and shrugged a bit.

Cheri shook her head before wandering towards another case full of brass cups. "I remember this one," she said, while pointing out the cup he'd shown her the night they had met.

Winston blurted out, "Oh yes, the drinking vessel from Marcus Galerius." He then turned to Algernon. "We think we know who he is."

Algernon chuckled. "Cheri already told me. He's a general that disappeared during the first invasion of Britannia in 55 BCE."

The curator looked back at Cheri, appearing a bit perturbed that someone once again had stolen his thunder, but soon he looked at her with more than mere academic interest. "So, where do you work?"

"Penton University in Ohio," Cheri admitted. "I work in special collections for the university's library, most of the time."

"She's getting her PhD in preservation," Algernon added, while drawing closer to her. He wrapped an arm around her waist to let Winston know he had a relationship with Cheri beyond the academic.

Cheri smiled at Winston. "So, what's in the next room, Dr. Walker?"

"I believe it will be the Weapons Room," Algernon replied, before Winston could answer, but it was Winston who led them into the adjoining room to their left, where gladii, spears, claymores, bows and arrows, longer swords, and a variety of daggers and knives decorated the walls and display cases. Some of the weaponry seemed ornate and must have been ceremonial, whereas other weapons looked as if they had shed blood in battle.

"Perhaps you two can answer why armor dated from the sixth century looks to be late Roman republic in style," Winston requested.

"That is another mystery which has not yet been solved," Algernon said with a chuckle. "Though, look at the armor," he said, while motioning to Cheri, who scrutinized the Roman-style armor.

Cheri stared intently at the metal plates. "Look at the dings, and that..." She paused. "Someone died in this," she whispered, pointing to a mended spot in the armor.

"Yes, we found tiny flakes of blood, there. We sent it to the lab," Algernon added, before staring at the mosaics which came from the site of a soldier in battle who held two swords.

"So, that is him, the man that wore this armor," Cheri asked while studying the mosaic.

"Yes, I'd like to think so," Algernon replied. "But then, I have to wonder about the enemy warriors he's facing. The ones clad in gold."

"They look Roman too," Winston commented. "Later period... late empire."

"It's interesting," Algernon admitted, forgetting his earlier annoyance with Walker. "We didn't find any gold there. Not a single coin! I mean how... who in the Celtic or Roman era didn't have gold to signify wealth? It's like these people or this man decided one day to simply switch all his wealth to silver."

Cheri grinned at him. "What I'd like to know is who were these people, I mean, some traders might have a foreign trinket or two, but why in Bath? It's such a big mishmash of cultures present here... like that fidchell set you showed me. How can there be such a center point of all this diversity?"

Algernon smiled at her and said, "I will... defer that question until after we've seen the entire exhibit." He chuckled.

Cheri smiled and then pouted.

"Shall we?" Winston asked, before walking ahead of them, still looking a bit dumbfounded.

After taking a few steps, Algernon felt Cheri grab his backside.

"You are such a tease," she whispered in his ear.

"I know," he murmured.

Cheri heard a cell phone alarm begin to peal and glanced over at Algernon, the source of the noise.

"It's me," he confirmed. "I need to get ready for the presentation, sorry Cheri." He approached her and smiled, before turning towards Dr. Walker. "Winston, would you mind continuing the tour with Cheri," he asked.

Cheri felt torn between seeing the rest of the exhibit and leaving with Algernon. She considered her options. "So, what's the next room," she asked.

The curator smiled and said, "The library. It's our display of all the scrolls."

Cheri uttered a subtle squeak of glee but then blushed a bit at the noise. "Okay, I have to see that."

"Oh, I suppose we could do that," Winston said with a chuckle.

Algernon pulled Cheri in for a kiss and whispered, "I'll save you a front seat."

"Thank you for everything," she replied. She watched Algernon grin and turn towards the exit, but then the sound of a throat clearing brought her focus back to her other escort.

"This way please," Dr. Walker drawled, while motioning for Cheri to follow him.

After trailing behind Dr. Walker down another corridor, they approached a guard waiting for them at the next door. She walked through the door and promptly gasped at the large number of aged scrolls presented along the walls and newer documents in the display cases. Some cards next to the scrolls translated the documents. At the opposite end of the room was a large glass enclosure holding a huge number of shelves and scroll cases.

Dr. Walker motioned her to the first display. "Here is the original catalog… well you would know these terms better than I. It's a listing of materials for this library in Bath and a description of what is included in the document and how the owner viewed the material. He, she, or they were most opinionated about some documents."

"It sounds like an annotated bibliography," Cheri said, while leaning in closer to stare down at the document. "This is the mother-load," she exclaimed, before realizing how inane she sounded. She giggled a little, out of her own nervousness. "This is just, thrilling."

"Yes, it is," her host agreed.

A series of scrolls caught her eye, and she walked towards them, but she could find no cards offering an explanation as to a translation of the document. "So, what are these about?"

Dr. Walker joined her in front of the scrolls and cleared his throat. "They had someone translate them, but they are written in some obscure Frankish dialect or some old form of German. Though, someone took notes on this in Old Irish. It's sort of like a college student scribbling notes in the margin of a textbook," he explained.

"But what do they say," Cheri asked again.

"We didn't want to worry our visitors. Together, they are something like a… grimoire," Dr. Walker admitted. "They discuss elemental magic, with primarily Irish and Celtic deities, and an alternate plane of existence." He laughed. "Some people would probably try to burn them. However, I do know they are from the ninth century, so they are relatively new documents for this collection."

"So, does this give any more clues about the librarian or keeper of this collection?"

"Oh, the infamous M.G.P.H scribbled his name on a few of these documents," answered the curator.

Cheri chuckled. "I'm willing to bet some old British noble wanted to show up his Saxon or Viking overlords and decided to take on the name of an ancestor."

"I've considered that myself," Walker said. "Perhaps the family decided to just keep using the name as a matter of pride. At least, that's what I think your... Algernon will probably use as reasoning in his presentation, if he mentions Galerius at all. Though to be honest, many will think it's all a massive forgery. However, I think as long as he doesn't draw any kind of conclusions from the dig, other than showing the findings, he'll have nothing to worry about."

Cheri nodded her head. "So, what's next?"

The curator rubbed his hands together. "Games and gambling!"

"Oh goody," Cheri blurted out with unrestrained joy.

*Great, now I feel like an idiot.*

Algernon had started memorizing the speech a few nights ago, but he still found himself needing his note cards. As he whispered the notes for each slide involved in the presentation, he noticed a group of students walking around testing the sound and visual equipment. Then he felt someone grab his lapel and began attaching a microphone to him, while another person passed over a bottle of water.

"Thanks," he said to everyone around him. While putting his opening thoughts in order, Algernon looked up and noticed Winston coming in from one of the wings. He walked over to his colleague, while attempting to stop feeling nervous. "Did Cheri enjoy the tour?"

"She most certainly did," Winston replied. "You've found yourself a smart one, Algernon. Smart and cute, you lucky bastard."

"I know," Algernon answered. "Did you find her a seat?"

"She's in the front. It was a little difficult. We owe you a big thank-you for giving your presentation here instead of Penton. We have people from the local academic community, as well as a few disheveled ones, who may be Nobel Laureates."

Algernon fell silent. After a pause, he said, "They're going to think I'm nuts."

"Well, just hit the highlights of what you found and don't mention Mr. Galerius," Winston suggested with a grin.

"I know... I won't."

"Dr. Walker, three minutes," a student with a clip-board and headset called, while another student grabbed Winston's lapel and attached a mini-microphone to it.

"It looks like you need to prep, too," Algernon remarked, thankful he had gotten there early so as to not feel rushed.

Winston chuckled. "No, I have it memorized, I think. Break a leg."

Algernon took one last look at his laptop and hoped this would be enough. He closed it and handed it over to one of the assistants. He insisted on wasting no thoughts on his stage fright. Instead, he tried to think over his favorite pieces in the collection.

Suddenly, the curtain rose, the lights hit him, and the music and applause washed over him. Algernon felt all eyes were upon him, as Winston began his introduction.

"And now," Winston grandstanded, "the man responsible for leading the team that located these remarkable finds, Dr. Algernon MacDonough!"

"Showtime," Algernon whispered to himself, as the room erupted in applause.

# chapter eight

orm glanced at the clock and saw that only a few seconds remained in the third period, in the midst of power play, as Yale remained short one man due to a recent penalty. As Norm looked on with a combination of anticipation and dread, one of the Yale players raced down the rink and lined his shot as the seconds ticked away. Two seconds remained when Norm's phone rang. While Norm looked down at his pocket out of habit, the stadium went wild.

*Crap! Mom always has the best timing.*

"What happened! What happened," he shouted in disbelief and shock while turning to Agnes, who joined the rest of the revelers in the celebrations.

"Yale won! Get up," she yelled as she pulled him up and embraced him, while his cell continued to peal.

He hugged Agnes but then pulled back. "Sorry, got to take this," he said to her in his best apologetic face, to which she nodded in response. He opened the cell, as he plugged his other ear with a finger. "Hi mom."

"What's that noise?"

*Mom usually forgets any kind of manners on the cellphone.*

"I'm at a hockey game."

"That's nice, dear. Chelsea told me that you and Cheri aren't together, is that true?" His mother's voice became tight.

"Yes, that's correct."

"Do you know what you're throwing away?"

"Mom," he said before sighing, "I don't want to have this conversation with you, right now."

"Alright, alright," his mother answered. "Shouldn't you give her and her family enough respect to say goodbye to her in person? I mean, you can't throw away your friendship with her, at least."

Norm paused. He and Cheri had known each other for a long time, granted but it wasn't like they were the best of friends. He decided it would be better to just do what had to be done. "Alright, mom. I'll see her when I get home."

At that moment, the noise began to die down, and Norm could hear his mother more clearly.

"Well, she's going to be at the Tappan's dinner party tonight." While the stadium noise had diminished, the line became filled with static.

"What is it," Agnes whispered.

Norm covered the mouthpiece. "I don't think I can get out of this," he informed her. "My parents want me to go to some dinner party hosted by that family we saw at the airport."

Agnes' face lit in a bemused smile. "My parents have asked me to do stranger things. When are we going?"

Norm grinned. "Mom, I'll be there as soon as I can.

"Okay. Be sure to wear your nice–"

The cell phone suddenly went to no bars.

Norm closed the phone, hoping he could remain incommunicado for now.

"You didn't even mention me," Agnes said with a pout.

He nearly started laughing. "If I told her that I was seeing someone else, she would flip out. I'd rather see that in person."

"So, my only purpose is to make your parents crazy?" Agnes grinned again, causing Norm to chuckle. "I love making parents crazy, especially mine," she added. "Though driving yours batty might be fun too." As Agnes embraced him, he leaned into her, smelling the scent of shampoo and fruit-scented lotion.

*God, I love her.*

Cheri followed the crowd towards the exhibits and the open bar. She tried to approach Algernon, but a group of people surrounded him and seemed to hang on his every word. She then felt herself pushed and shoved into Dr. Walker. "Sorry," she muttered to him, feeling embarrassed.

"No problem," he replied, looking as if he were embarrassed as well. "So, did you enjoy the presentation?"

"Yes," Cheri answered while nodding her head, "but I haven't even had an opportunity to tell him."

"Well, the groupies and remoras have attached themselves, now," Dr. Walker said with a smirk. "Hmmm, if you like, I think I can distract them, if you want to escape. We do have an exhibit hall that's not open. It's quiet in there, and you can… congratulate him."

"Why?" She raised a brow at him.

"Honestly," Dr. Walker answered while staring at the floors for a moment, "we have a budget crunch, like every other educational institution. However, this exhibit is gathering interest, and interest means more donations and more people coming to school here. I'll let Algie break a rule or two for that. Besides that, look at him. He's a little scared of all the attention."

"Thanks," Cheri whispered.

"It's down the hall to the right. 3920 is the code to get in."

"3920," Cheri repeated.

"I'll find something shiny to toss at them, and he'll meet you there."

Cheri leaned in and kissed Dr. Walker's cheek, before walking down the main hall. She studied the names of the exhibit hall rooms as she walked down the hall, making note of the rooms Algernon had shown her before, namely the game room, the vault, and the library, but she soon came to the last door of the main hall, which bore no identifying sign, except for 'not open to the public'. Once at the recommended door, she entered the code, which gave her a satisfying beep. She then opened the door and walked into the exhibit hall. Once inside the dark room, Cheri turned around and slid her hands along the walls, searching for a light switch. After a few moments of fumbling and cussing under her breath, she found the switches and turned on the lights.

The room lights bathed the exhibit hall room in warm brilliance.

Based on her examination the room's contents, she would probably classify this exhibit as being the 'bedroom'. In this room, the display cases held a large collection of Sheela-na-gigs and phalluses. Mosaics of frolicking mythical figures, as well as what appeared to be mortals, graced sections of a wall that were part of the exhibit. There seemed to be old glass bottles and other knick-knacks on shelves and a few tables.

While contemplating a rather large polished black phallus, which looked to be hewn from fine black marble, she heard the door open, and Cheri turned to see Algernon entering the exhibit hall and closing the door behind him. "So, is this part of the exhibit," Cheri asked.

His eyes widened for a moment, and he smiled with his lips curling in a sensuous movement. Algernon held two champagne flutes in one hand and an opened bottle in the other. "It will be, as soon as it's finished," he said before crossing the room over to her. "It wasn't quite ready. Plus, we have to be prepared to explain all of this to a somewhat prudish audience." He began to pour them champagne and started to hand her a glass, but then he stopped and looked at her. "You have to promise first not overdo the champagne. We do have to get you to the party, later."

Cheri smirked. "I'll behave," she teased, before snatching the glass of champagne away from Algernon, causing a bit of a spill. "Sorry. A toast, to your presentation! You were brilliant," she said, meeting his dark eyes. "I'm flattered I was here to listen to your speech."

His fingers entwined with hers. "I'm flattered as well."

They both sipped at their champagne.

"Truth be told," Algernon added, "I asked them to delay opening this part of the exhibit."

"Really? Why," she asked, giggling a little.

"So we could do this." Algernon took her glass and set it down on one of the tables. His hands caressed her face, and he stared into her eyes before kissing her.

Cheri noticed his scent of musk and wild citrus overwhelmed the smell of aged documents and artifacts with the hint of tweedyness that seemed to blossom around Yale. She lost track of rational thoughts as she found herself pushed up against a table then on top of it with his mouth caressing hers.

Algernon's reached his hands under her skirt and nimbly slid off her panties, which wound up tucked into one of his pockets.

She attempted to stroke Algernon's groin, but she gave up as soon as she realized she couldn't seem to reach that area with him pressed against her. Cheri decided instead to just to try unzipping him and getting his belt off. As she fumbled with his belt, Cheri thought back to that first night they had met, wondering whether they'd be interrupted again, and if that were the case, whether they would be able to stop, this time.

Algernon raised himself, making it easier for her to work his belt and unzip his pants.

In no time, she held his substantial length in her digits. With her focus on the moment to come, the sounds of the other people at the exhibit hall in the public areas faded, and she could hear nothing more than the two of them. Then she had to lift her arms, as Algernon slid off her shirt, which he tossed across the room.

Algernon brought his head close to her neck and began to nuzzle her throat with his mouth, while his fingers probed and rubbed her sex.

Caught in the throws of his caress, Cheri feverishly patted down his pockets, hoping to find wrapped condoms.

*Shit, did we forgot protection again?*

Cheri uttered a moan, forgetting condoms for a moment, as he continued to nip at her and finger her playfully.

Algernon unfastened her bra and began to massage her breasts, and then his heated fingers, wet with her essence, stroked her back.

She felt his hands slide back to her hips, down her mound, and into her crevasse. Her fervor intensified, and she arched towards Algernon. As she writhed in the midst his tactile probing, Cheri witnessed him toss a shiny foil packet onto the table, causing her to inhale with relief. "You are a life saver. Let me get this on you," she gasped.

Algernon withdrew his fingers and pulled back a bit, allowing Cheri to grab the condom. "I remembered, after our last encounter."

As Cheri removed the prophylactic from its wrapper, she cooed, "ooo... I love a man who comes prepared. Now, let me get this on you." She crouched down and began to fluff his member. She thought about using her mouth to apply the condom but decided against it, owing to her failure training on a cucumber. Instead, she used her hands, careful to unroll the item completely.

Immediately after sheathing the condom over Algernon, he lifted her up onto the desk and penetrated her.

She wrapped her legs around his waist and began meeting his thrusts. As they writhed against each other, she felt her pleasure build with each movement. In a short span of time, Cheri's passion threatened to overwhelm her, and then she gave in, moaning in ecstasy, giving up what remained of her control and worries about being in a somewhat public place, surrounded by what amounted to an ancient sex toy collection.

Algernon moaned while caressing her hair, and then she felt him stiffen in release as he started to come, each burst matching with hers.

She sucked in lung-fulls of air as spasms of delight rocketed through her, as her own release made her shudder and utter his name.

After filling the condom inside of her with his seed, Algernon rested against her with his hands cradling her.

Cheri closed her eyes, feeling cherished and blessed.

Several minutes after experiencing coital bliss with the woman he loved, and after cleaning up as best as he could in the employee wash room, Algernon reclined in the back seat of the car they had hired, as Cheri leaned against his shoulder nuzzling his cheek with hers, while traveling through New Haven.

"This has been so wonderful," she purred in the manner of a highly satisfied feline. She slid one of her legs over his.

"It's been my pleasure," he said, while leaning in closer to her. One of his hands crept down her lifted leg to slide teasingly under her skirt. He fingered her mercilessly through her panties.

"I'm so sorry that I have to ruin the evening by dragging you to some bloody party at my parents. Wait... let's just forget the whole thing." She sighed, as her prior thoughts echoed in her head, only to be drowned out by the stern visage of her mother's face yelling about how disrespectful she was. "Never mind. Mom would call. Then she'd guilt me. I know. I'll pop in, say 'hi'. You can wait here in the car, and I'll come back out after a few minutes. Then we can go back to the hotel, order room service, and watch crappy hotel TV."

Algernon mused for a moment that this solution could work, but then he noticed Cheri's hazel eyes staring blankly at the passenger door next to him. He withdrew his fingers from her nethers to let her think straight.

"Oh, but that wouldn't work. My parents would insist on my staying longer. I could ask the driver to take you back and get a cab back to the hotel."

He was about to agree, when she met his eyes, which looked almost fearful.

*Could her parents be all that bad? Probably not.*

"Cheri," he cooed, while smoothing a hand over her frizzing hair, which seemed to reflect her mood at this very moment.

"Yes?"

"I'd be honored to meet your parents."

*I am not exactly being truthful, here, but it is obvious she needs me. This feels right.*

"You would–"

Relief shone in her eyes.

"Yes. You don't think I'm nice enough to meet them," he asked, while making an obvious effort to pout a bit in a playful fashion.

Cheri chuckled a little. "No. You're not the problem. I just haven't exactly told them about you."

He pulled away, feeling a little hurt with her honesty.

"Oh no, no, it's not you, Algernon." Cheri looked crestfallen, now. "My parents thought I was dating this other guy. They were expecting me to show up with him. For me to show up with someone else would... would..." Her eyes grew hazy in thought, before brightening suddenly as if lit up by a brilliant idea or realization... an epiphany, even. "They would be devastated! Oh, this is going to be great!" She grinned in an almost a demented way.

"I don't think I'm that much of a letdown," he chuckled a little, though he was curious about the sudden change in her mood.

"Sorry, but you're an intelligent, gorgeous foreigner with facial hair," Cheri announced while grinning. "They'll think it's a travesty!"

Algernon smirked, surprised and confused by her gleeful outburst and reasoning. "So, this is a good thing?"

"Absolutely," she cheered, before leaning in and kissing him.

He felt his passion for her rising.

Cheri looked up as the car turned. "Well this is it," she muttered.

Mansions and large homes decorated the tree-lined streets.

As the car pulled into a large driveway, Algernon observed that the house didn't look too scary.

After the car stopped, Cheri pulled away from him. She ran her hands over her hair but still managed to look a little worried.

The driver then opened her door, and Cheri stepped out.

Algernon slid out behind her and then handed over a worn business card to the driver. "Could you pick us up in about two hours?"

"No problem," the driver said, nodding to him.

Algernon turned back to regard Cheri, who still managed to look a little worried. As the engine started up again, he took her hand and caressed it. "It's not too late to leave."

Cheri hesitated as if waiting, wanting her escape route to close. While she waited, the car backed out of the driveway and disappeared down the street. "But the car left already," Cheri whispered ironically, since she had ample time to signal the driver to wait.

Willing to suggest some other escape, not sure whether she was eager to face her parents or run off, he said, "We can hitch a ride, then."

"Oh, good one," Cheri chuckled. "In this neighborhood, they'll set the dogs out on us."

"Well, we foreigners can have a sense of humor, once in awhile," he said while winking at her.

*Phhhew... I'm glad she didn't seriously consider that suggestion... what was I thinking?*

"Well, it's now or never," she said, before grasping his hand and leading him to the door.

*Why am I doing this to Algernon and me?*

Cheri walked with him to the front door, which opened suddenly, revealing a man wearing a caterer's uniform.

"Cheri Tappan and... guest," Cheri announced, while grinning at Algernon.

"Please, come in."

She led Algernon through the front entry of the house.

A few familiar people and a large crowd of strangers mingled through the house while holding glasses of wine and talking to each other. Background music, possibly Brahms or Beethoven, drifted in through stereo speakers in every room.

*Who am I kidding... mom and dad probably have the Yale School Of Music chamber orchestra upstairs or in another room downstairs and are piping the music through the house... so like them.*

"Mom's upgraded," she said, noticing changes, like new fixtures and updated furniture throughout the house.

*Where did the curio cabinet and the knick-knacks I grew up with go?*

Cheri frowned as she stared at the new furnishings.

"You have a lovely home," Algernon murmured.

Cheri felt her face heat as she thought about what was missing. She turned back to look at Algernon. "Sorry," she admitted. "I forgot... I was lost in thought. I didn't grow up, here. I don't even remember most of the furniture or art in this house." She felt a tight grimace curve her features. "My parents weren't so socially elite in my childhood."

"So, they re-invented themselves," he asked. "At least they aren't in the poorhouse. I'm sure you're proud of them a little."

Cheri chewed on the sentiment for a few moments. "I just worry that they don't remember who they were. I liked them, then. Now, I don't think I know them."

Algernon wrapped an arm around her. "I'm sure they're proud of you and love you."

"One would hope," she muttered.

"So, where are your parents," Algernon asked.

Cheri considered that she had spent the last few minutes actively hiding from her family. With her mind now set to confront her parents instead of avoid them, she listened to telltale signs of their presence. After only a few seconds, she could hear someone speaking in loud Italian in the distance.

*There you are, mother.*

She rolled her eyes.

"What is it?"

Cheri turned back to Algernon. "So, do you want to meet my mother?"

"If you're still game..." His eyes promised methods of escape existed if she wished.

*But escape is not an option.*

Cheri inhaled and exhaled, hoping to center herself, preparing for the battle of wills in which she was soon to be engaged. "Then, follow me to the 'cucina', as my mom would call our kitchen." She took Algernon's hand and weaved their way through the crowds, recognizing more faces the closer they approached ground zero. Mouths opened and closed, but she ignored their greetings, focused as she was on her quarry. Soon, the pack of visitors became dense, so much so that Cheri lost her grip on Algernon and watched him disappear into the throng. She could hear more Italian about something involving food... capers, perhaps, but she turned away from the hunt, deciding to go find Algernon, when the most grating voice to ever utter her least-desired nickname pierced the din of the crowd, causing all other talking to cease for a moment.

"Pumpkin! You gave me such a fright!"

Cheri uttered an inward groan, before turning to face her mother, who smiled and extended her arms towards Cheri whilst holding a half-empty martini glass.

Her mother's bob-length hair now appeared to be darker, but her eyes remained a sparkling hazel. "Now come and give your mom a hug! You're late."

Cheri embraced her mother, and then her mother backed away, holding her hands.

By now, the din of conversation around them resumed but remained at a reasonable level for her to hear polite conversation.

"Look at you," her mother drawled. "Don't you look... smart!"

Cheri blushed again. She then clenched up well, knowing she was about to receive a full-on onslaught of guilt wielded as wickedly as a berserker's axe though with the precision of a neurosurgeon.

"So, you finally decided to come home. We're so glad to have you visit. We have your room all set up. I'm sure I can convince your professors to let you stay here, awhile. Surely you can complete some of your work online. Where are your bags, pumpkin?"

Her mother's first attack drew blood, so to speak, but Cheri was prepared. She countered by parrying her mother's attacks. "I'm staying at the hotel, mom. I can't stay for weeks. I've got to get back to work."

Undaunted, her mother launched into another salvo. "Oh, come on, pumpkin. Stay here and apply to work at Yale. You've been wanting to work at Yale since you were four... or some ridiculous age."

This stratagem caught Cheri off balance and on her back foot. She tried to think of something to say, as her mother sipped at her martini, but nothing manifested itself right away.

*I do want to work at Yale, but I will never admit it to mom. She would never let up!*

Cheri's mom changed tactics. "I sense this is still a touchy subject," her mother said, before putting down her glass. She embraced Cheri again. "Still, it's so wonderful to have you here. So, tell your mother why you broke up with–"

Cheri witnessed her mother turn her face towards the crowd, only to reveal Norm sipping on a glass of wine. "Shit," she whispered to herself.

Algernon felt like flotsam, as strangers pushed past him and pulled him away from Cheri. He soon found himself surrounded by people who sounded and looked like investment bankers, or something involving finances. A vortex of boredom surrounded him, as they tried to entice him into a conversation about futures. But before he had lost all hope of finding someone with which to engage in intelligent conversation, an arm draped around his shoulders whisked him away from the vortex of boredom. He soon realized the assistance came from an unexpected source.

"Uncle Al, what are you doing here?" Agnes grinned. "You're not checking on me, are you?"

He felt a little insulted and embarrassed for Agnes at hearing the whispered phrase of 'trophy girl' from the group of investment bankers he had just escaped.

*Didn't these people hear 'Uncle Al'?*

"Where am I dragging you again," Agnes asked.

"Further away from the vortex of boredom, if you please," he said.

Agnes chuckled. "Now you know how I feel when you and your friends drag me into conversations about history and archeology."

Algernon bit his lower lip. "Are my conversations that dull?"

"Well, only slightly less so than investment banking," Agnes admitted. "Seriously, though, why are you here?"

"Ehm, I came here with Cheri after the presentation."

"That explains things," Agnes said, before releasing his arm, as they reached a quiet corner.

"What things," he asked.

But before she could answer, a loud, feminine voice pierced the room.

"NORM!"

He and his niece turned to look at the woman.

Norm choked a bit on the wine as someone shouted his name, causing shivers to surge up and down his spine. He looked up to see Chelsea Tappan gliding toward him. He didn't feel quite ready to handle Cheri's mother at this point. After all, he had dumped her daughter, and Chelsea could come on a little strong. He turned, hoping to sneak out, but then a feminine hand touched his shoulder. Norm turned and found himself wrapped up in a hug, engulfed in a mixture of scents, including heavy perfume and expensive alcohol. The embrace was a bit more intimate than he desired, especially since he used to have a crush on Mrs. Tappan.

*As a teenager, I remember those pool parties, where she would come out in her bikini... and oh. I don't need that thought right now. Go away!*

A wet kiss on his cheek made his discomfort increase.

"Oh, my favorite son-in-law to never be," Chelsea drawled. "Is there no hope for you and my pumpkin?"

Norm looked past Chelsea and noticed Cheri, who looked perturbed. He didn't expect to be tag-teamed. Then he heard his own mother and felt his annoyance rise.

"Normie! Where have you been?" Mrs. Tappan released him, and then he found himself in his mother's arms.

*Crap!*

His mother dragged him towards Cheri.

"It's so good to see you again, sweetie," she said sweetly, as she embraced his friend. A fake smile remained on his mother's face, but her eyes revealed her true fury. His mother pulled away from Cheri and said, "I was so heartbroken when Normie made up this horrible story about you two not seeing each other any more." His mother's smile grew brighter. "Now, I see you here with Norm, and everything is as right as rain."

Cheri uttered a sound of utter annoyance, almost a scream. "Norm and I decided to go our separate ways!"

All other sound in the house ceased.

Norm could feel all eyes focus on him and Cheri. He remembered wanting to discuss this calmly, but no, now he was surrounded by she-wolves. All the alpha-females prepared to attack him and tear him to pieces.

"Look, you three just stop. Don't escalate this. Cheri, would you please walk with me outside?"

Chelsea backed away, and his mother stared at him in shock.

Cheri's mouth remained open, but instead of arguing, she acquiesced. "Okay," she squeaked.

Norm grabbed her arm and pulled her through the crowd. On their way out, the murmuring began anew.

He vaguely remembered his parents mentioning some backyard with beautiful landscaping, not to mention a pool and hot tub. He reasoned they could find peace in the backyard. He headed out a back door, towards the pool, and over to a bench he found.

Cheri's hand remained in his.

Norm felt some shock that she hadn't pulled away.

Norm sat down on the bench.

Cheri joined him, and together they stared at the pool.

After a protracted silence, Norm chose to speak first. "I'm sorry for my mother's conduct. She was way out of line," he said to Cheri.

Her eyes turned up to him. "It's okay. I'm sure our… breakup came as a bit of a shock to her."

Norm smirked for a moment. "I'm just glad your dad and mine were upstairs in the model train room."

"Oh, is that where they were? Yeah, he tends to fly off the handle, too," Cheri agreed. She looked away from Norm and stared at the pool.

He felt wistful for a moment. "So, was the whole friendship thing between us way back when so horrible?"

Cheri shrugged a bit. "We were young and stupid, both of us." Her eyes rested on his again. "I guess we became two very different people, and we weren't mature about it."

Norm shook his head a little. "I think we know that maturity came on slower for me."

Cheri uttered a chuckle. "Yeah, you're kind of an asshole, sometimes."

"And chauvinistic, condescending, manipulative–"

"You're not really manipulative, Norm. That's something our mothers excel at." She studied him for a moment. "You're not just saying this," she said.

"I'm not trying to get into your knickers," he replied, while holding up his hands. "Clearly, you and I aren't meant for coupledom, couplehood, whatever. If I'd known that in high school, our friendship wouldn't be at the edge of a crevasse, now. Then again, I was a hornball in high school."

Cheri shifted a bit to face him and exhaled as if she were trying to find words.

"Well, it doesn't have to hurtle off the crevasse, Norm. We have known each other for almost all our lives."

He felt a little warmth at those words. "Do you really think there's hope for us to remain friends? I'd hate to throw that away." Norm rotated his body to face her.

Cheri's face and body relaxed. "I think so. It'll take some work."

"I know," he admitted. "I'm willing to do what I need to keep you as a friend."

Cheri smiled. "I'd like that."

He smiled back at her.

*This is more than I could have hoped for.*

## chapter nine

ome on, Uncle Al. She'll hurt him, and we have to do something," Agnes shouted as she continued to drag him towards the backyard.

"Why are you dragging me?"

Agnes turned back to him. "We have to do something."

"And what do you expect me to do," Algernon asked Agnes.

"Argh!" She made a noise of consternation, a little softer than the noise Cheri made earlier.

"Fine," Agnes whined, continuing in her rant. "I'll do it myself," she muttered, before storming off.

Algernon looked around the room and noticed he was on the periphery of another great void, though this time, instead of investment bankers, two rather prominent women stood in the middle of the room, frowning.

*Two magnificent hens vying for dominance? Or something else...*

One of the women, who looked a little like Cheri... presumably her mother, sipped at a martini glass between delivering talking points. He reasoned that the other woman must be Norm's mother. The two women seemed to be speaking politely to each other, but Algernon sensed the tension in the room.

He realized that they must have planned for their children to show up at this party as a couple. Since he had somewhat of an idea as to what was going on, he felt a strange need to diffuse things. He walked over to the women, feeling a desire to introduce himself, and cleared his throat. "Pardon me, Mrs. Tappan?"

The woman with the half-empty martini glass turned her hazel eyes towards him.

*This woman and Cheri both share similar features. I think this is Cheri's mother, alright.*

A moment of annoyance at his interruption resided in her eyes, but then she turned on the charm and beamed at him. "Yes?"

The other woman seemed to fade away from the conversation.

"I'm Algernon MacDonough," he began. "I just wanted to introduce myself to you."

"Oh, I'm very pleased to make your acquaintance. I'm Chelsea." Cheri's mother extended a hand to him. "Forgive me, but have we met before? Your name rings with familiarity." Chelsea smiled at him again.

Just then, Algernon felt a firm hand on his shoulder and heard a very familiar but unexpected voice close to his ear.

"Chelsea, it's great to see you again."

"Uhm… Winston," Chelsea greeted, before turning her radiance towards Algernon's colleague. She leaned in to kiss his cheek.

"I see you just have met the astounding Dr. MacDonough," Winston said.

"Oh, another doctor," Chelsea trilled.

"I'm not exactly astounding," Algernon admitted.

"Oh, such modesty," Winston admonished with a chuckle. "You remember the exhibit from Bath, England?"

"Of course," Chelsea answered. "I'm so sorry that I missed the soiree tonight. I had this little celebration to deal with. Did everything go well with the exhibit," she asked.

"It went extremely well," Winston replied. "Dr. MacDonough found the artifacts that were shown at the exhibit."

Chelsea's smile changed from a fake façade to true and genuine reflection of affection. "Oh, truly?"

"Yes. His presentation was our highest attended event in the last fifteen, maybe twenty, years," Winston replied.

Algernon felt a little surprised that Chelsea knew about the event.

His expression must have revealed that to their hostess as she leaned forward and placed a gentle and well-manicured hand on his. "I'm a board member for Yale's museums," she said to Algernon.

"So, you signed my check," he said, laughing at this strange circumstance.

"Yes, that's me," Chelsea chuckled. "Now, Dr. Mac… Algernon," Chelsea continued. "You have to tell me about the bedroom exhibit. Is it true about all those naughty toys in there?"

"Oh yes, absolutely," he answered. "There is quite the collection of phalluses in there. Though, they weren't generally thought of as toys–"

"Oh, you must tell me more," Chelsea giggled.

At that moment, he felt a light touch slide over his back. He turned and saw Cheri, who wrapped him in an embrace. Algernon witnessed surprise on Chelsea's face.

Cheri rested her finger on his chin for a moment and stood up on her tiptoes to kiss him deeply.

It surprised him, a little. He forgot himself and wrapped his arms around Cheri, but then realizing Cheri's mother stood before them, he pulled away in embarrassment.

Cheri turned to her mother. "Mom, this is my boyfriend, Algernon."

Chelsea's shock seemed to melt away into approval.

At the same time, he could hear Agnes introducing herself to Mrs. Bradley with charm and grace. The two women seemed to take to each other.

Chelsea made a little squealing sound of excitement. "Oh, my pumpkin never tells us anything!" She then wrapped an arm around him and Cheri. "We all need to get better acquainted, Algernon," Chelsea said. "Would you like something to drink? A good single malt perhaps? We have some old stuff in the den for this occasion." She motioned for a waiter, who approached. "We need the Highland Park Orcadian 1964 vintage and three glasses," she informed him, before turning back to her guests. "Let's go someplace less noisy."

Cheri's relief over the night's occurrences allowed her to relax in bed next to Algernon. She exhaled and smiled as she lay on her back. However, something in the back of her mind woke her around one in the morning. After reassuring herself that her parents seemed happy about a decision she had made, she pounced on Algernon, who still appeared to be recovering.

Algernon turned to face her. "So, what brought this on?" he asked.

Cheri turned her eyes towards him. "My parents are happy and told me so. I realize it sounds stupid, but most of the time they complain about all of my choices."

He shifted onto his side and played with a strand of her hair. "Praise in your family must be very rare," he said, before kissing her brow.

"I thought the species died off when I was about three," she admitted.

"Well, that explains everything. I'm so glad I was able to meet them both."

"Me too," she said, stroking a finger over his chest. "I'm more surprised that my dad came out of hiding." She turned on her side to look at him better.

Algernon scooted in closer to Cheri. "Well, it's nice to know that I'm not the only one who feels that way about large parties."

"I couldn't have faced them alone, so thank you for coming in. How am I ever going to make that up to you?" Cheri pulled aside the sheets and began nibbling her way down his chest. She sensed him tense as she licked at a ticklish spot. At that moment, she heard a cellphone begin to ring, but this time she ignored it and continued down his stomach.

Unfortunately, the phone continued ringing.

Algernon uttered a sound of annoyance and began cursing in some other language. He looked at the phone and then picked it up, seeming to recognize the number.

"Winston, it's nearly two in the morning. What is it?" Algernon fell silent, though Cheri could hear excited mumbling through the phone. "What?! When did this happen? Do they know who did it?"

Cheri sat up, spooked. "What hap–"

Algernon waved her off, and she fell silent. "How could they have done such a thing? That's impossible, Winston."

She watched Algernon's incredulity turn to resignation.

"Okay, okay. I'm on my way." He closed his phone and stood up, letting the phone fall from his fingers to hit the carpeted floor.

"What is it? What's wrong," she asked.

Anxiety reflected in Algernon's eyes. "Get dressed," he said. "We're going back to the museum."

Cheri's heart raced as the cab neared the university. Upon arrival, she began counting the police cars with their colorful flashing lights.

*Who knew New Haven would have so many cops?*

In her reflection in the window, she could see questioning in her eyes. Algernon's agitation did not decrease as they neared the museum.

She caught his eyes and opened her mouth again.

"I just have to see this with my own eyes," he said.

The cab slowed down, upon approaching a young officer.

Algernon turned towards the officer and lowered the window.

The officer leaned toward the open window as Algernon handed over his identification. "Dr. MacDonough," the officer said, while nodding his head. "We're expecting you. Please proceed to the parking lot. Special Agent Winchester is waiting for you at the main entrance of the museum." He then motioned some other officers to move the roadblock before stepping away from the cab.

Cheri shuddered as several officers wearing bulletproof vests ran by.

The cab finally reached the front of the museum, and the driver parked. The cabbie turned back to face them and said, "Just get out of my cab. Ask the cops for a ride back."

Algernon stared at the cabbie and shrugged. He stepped out and offered Cheri a hand.

As soon as Cheri got out and closed the door, the cab peeled away, with tires screeching.

Algernon dropped her hand and practically raced towards a group of men wearing FBI jackets.

A young agent turned to face Algernon. "You Dr. MacDonough?"

Algernon stopped and nodded, just as she caught up to them.

"I'm Agent Winchester. That's agents Hurt and Dawson," the agent said, with a slight inclination of his head.

"I have to see it," Algernon demanded.

The Agent nodded. "We anticipated that. I'll take you there myself."

Cheri began to follow him, but then Hurt or Dawson stepped between her and Algernon.

"Sorry, ma'am. You'll have to wait. This is a crime scene," one of them ordered.

"That's Dr. Tappan, my assistant," Algernon argued. "I need her help identifying the missing objects."

Cheri tried to keep her mouth shut as the other agent shrugged and stepped aside. She followed Algernon and Winchester into the building. She felt a gnawing fear that there might be bodies in the museum, yet everything looked so calm. Other scenarios ran through her head.

*Vandals? Drunk intellectuals from the exhibit? But Algernon said exhibits were missing... burglars!*

"How was it first discovered," Algernon asked agent Winchester.

"Security Officer Beam discovered it," Winchester answered, while ushering them towards one of the exhibit rooms.

"Did the alarms go off," Cheri asked upon finding her voice.

"We don't know," Winchester replied.

"You don't," Algernon asked as he glanced around the room. "This is a very secure museum, or at least that's what Winston said."

"We still don't know what happened. The system was never tripped. We can't explain it," Winchester added, while rubbing his hands together.

Cheri chimed in again. "What about the cameras? Don't they have security…"

*Oh crap! Somebody probably has a sex tape of me and Algernon!*

Winchester turned towards her. "We checked the tapes. The ones in the active exhibit halls went dark."

"So, did someone disconnect them or spray-paint them?" Algernon asked, while still managing to sound panicked.

"No, they weren't touched. They just recorded absolute darkness." The agent shrugged a little. "I'll show you two what's left of the exhibits. I need you two and Dr. Walker to give me an itemized list of what's missing later."

Cheri braced herself for the worst as she walked through the doors of the first exhibit hall. She expected to see glass shattered and trash scattered, yet the floors remained clean. She then noticed that all the coins remained in the display boxes and that only a few items of jewelry seemed to be gone. She wondered how the thieves managed to remove the artifacts without cutting or breaking the glass.

"The sapphire necklace and the jade earrings are gone, as are the silver torcs," Algernon noted. He stopped in front of a display. "But, here are the pearl necklaces." He sounded confused.

Winchester nodded. "Shall we go to the next exhibit room?"

Cheri began making mental notes on the missing pieces. The fidchell board and set, the cups, a few pieces of jewelry, some of the weapons, and the armor appeared to be absent. It almost seemed that someone picked out the personal or controversial pieces.

Cheri and Algernon continued following Winchester through the doors to the closed 'bedroom' exhibit.

Algernon remained silent and distant as he stared at empty spots that once contained his treasures.

"Is there anything I can do to help," she asked.

Algernon looked over at her and then turned back to Winchester. "Could you give us a moment?"

Winchester nodded. "Sure," he replied before walking out of the exhibit hall.

Cheri opened her arms, embraced Algernon, and kissed his lips.

He pulled her in closer and then broke off the kiss, resting his sweaty forehead against her shoulder. "I can't believe this," he whispered. "What am I going to do, Cheri?"

She stroked his dark hair and closed her eyes for a moment. "It's mind-boggling that they could take these things and not be discovered," she murmured to him, not wanting to admit that she loved the feel of his facial hair against her neck and cheek.

"They seemed to know which artifacts were the most controversial pieces," he added.

"I'm..." she paused. "Maybe it's more than that. The ones that are gone, they seem personal."

He pulled back and saw a look in his eyes. "I didn't want to admit that," he said, "but you are right, I think."

"So what do we do now," she asked. Though she would love to stay and help Algernon, she had to fly back later this morning and get back to work this afternoon. Also, mid-term projects were due in Dr. Reynolds' classes soon, and that meant extra grading work for her.

Algernon swiped an arm over his brow. "I have to stay until we're done. I would miss the flight, I think."

She moved into his arms again, as Algernon nuzzled her neck. "I understand," she said. "I wish there was more time for us, but I know that we'll have time soon."

His hands ran over her unkempt hair. "I'll call you when I get back in town."

"No," she answered with a smile. "You will call me tonight when you get back to the hotel. You will call me every damn day until you get home, and then you'll call me again, Algernon."

His eyes wrinkled and his lips curled up in a smile. Algernon kissed her again. "You should probably get back to bed," he informed her, while running his hands up and down her arms.

Cheri smiled at him. "I know. I love you." She wondered if she should feel nervous admitting it, but it felt right.

"I love you too," he said.

They shared one more kiss, but then a knock at the door prompted them to pull away.

"Am I interrupting," Agent Winchester queried while leaning in the door.

Algernon shook his head. "Dr. Tappan is heading back to Penton tomorrow to handle my classes. Could you give her a ride back to the hotel?"

Winchester turned away and yelled, "Dawson! Dr. Tappan needs a ride to the hotel."

Agent Dawson appeared in the doorway and beckoned to Cheri. "This way, ma'am."

"Thank you, Agent Dawson." Cheri walked to the doorway to follow the agent out to his car, but before she left the room, she looked back to Algernon, wishing she could continue to comfort him, but that seemed impossible at the moment.

# chapter ten

fter a sleepless morning, Cheri found herself at the airport ticket kiosk. She blinked, wishing for a decent cup of coffee and donut and realized that she was in the line for the second class baggage drop off. She considered going to the first-class line, but only two other people stood in front of her at this point.

"Cheri," a female voice shouted behind her. She turned and noticed Agnes and Norm standing in line behind her.

Agnes pulled her in for a hug, radiating brilliant happiness, while Norm looked quite pleased himself.

"We heard about the theft at the exhibit. Uncle Al is really upset." Agnes' smile faded.

"Yes, lots of interesting pieces disappeared," Cheri answered.

"It's a shame that you have to travel home alone," Agnes said, appearing even sadder. "Uncle Al said he was really wishing he could spend more time with you."

"Oh, it'll be fine, Agnes," Cheri said. "He has to stay here and make sure the feds know what to look for." She squeezed Agnes' hand. She then studied Norm and Agnes again. "You two do make a beautiful couple. It's a horrible cliché, I know, but it's true."

The line move forward, so Cheri scooted her stuff ahead, with Norm and Agnes following. When the person in front of her got to the counter, the first agent became available. An agent, a young woman wearing the gray and blue vest, motioned for Cheri to approach.

As Cheri placed her bags on the scale, the woman smiled at her and asked, "Name and destination, please."

As Cheri pulled out her ID, she looked at Norm and Agnes standing close together. She then turned back to the ticket agent and passed over her ID.

The agent compared her ID with her computer screen and checked the baggage ribbon Cheri had gotten from the kiosk. "Ms. Tappan, you're booked on flight number 162. First class, row B, seat number 1."

"Miss," Cheri said to the agent, "my traveling companion won't be joining us, so I was wondering whether I could swap these tickets I have with someone else on this flight."

The agent's eyes became saucers. "This is a joke, right?"

"No. I'm serious. Can we do it?"

"Sure, if they agree to it." The agent snorted a little.

"Agnes, Norm," she said while looking at the couple over her shoulder. "Bring up your luggage."

"What's up," Agnes asked as they reached the counter.

Cheri grinned, feeling a bit of her disappointment fade. "How would you two like to be in first class?"

The surprise on their faces was priceless.

Algernon lost track of the time. His internal clock believed it was nearly eight in the evening, but who knew. He did know that he should probably call Cheri soon.

*She might be home, by now, or at work... Did she have to go to work this afternoon, or is that tomorrow? I'm too tired to think clearly. The g-men left for dinner, promising to bring me Pad Se Ew with chicken from the Thai place, but who knows whether they will remember.*

Algernon yawned as he started to sort through the photos of the missing exhibits, but he looked up when he noticed Winston walking in with two cups of coffee.

"Sorry Algernon. This is utter shite, but at least it's caffeinated."

"Thanks." Algernon removed his reading glasses and rubbed his eyes. He extended an arm towards the curator and received a Styrofoam cup of hot brine. As he took a sip, Algernon tried not to make a face at the sludgy mixture of grounds and water.

"You're welcome," Walker said before sitting down at the table across from him. He pulled out his glasses and donned them. "Well, the insurance underwriters have left. They seem very upset that there's no evidence or clues to explain how this catastrophe happened or who did it." He took a sip of his own coffee and shuddered. "They practically accused me of orchestrating the theft myself."

Algernon set down the cup and noticed the photo of the fidchell board. "This is no inside job, Winston."

"I know," Winston said with a chuckle. He stood up and stretched. "You know what I think, Algernon?"

"What?"

Winston picked up the photo of the fidchell board. "I bet that Mr. Galerius came back from the grave to reclaim it." His smile turned mischievous. "Now, we just need to interview every ghost we can find."

Algernon started laughing, and his associate joined in.

A buzzing sound coming from Winston prompted him to pull out his cellphone. He looked at the screen and said, "Well, that's the third text I got. Apparently, if I don't get home soon, the dog will get my dinner. You want to join me for leftovers?"

Algernon shuddered, thinking of Marybeth's cooking. "I'm going to go through the catalogs again, just to make sure we're not missing anything."

"Alright... just don't stay up all night with the... ghooooosts," Winston murmured, before picking up his cup and leaving the room.

Algernon rolled his eyes after Winston left and pulled out his glasses. As he took another sip of the godawful drek in his cup, he noticed that the lights in the room appeared to be dimming.

He shouted, "Winston, this isn't funny. Quit clowning around," but the lights continued to dim, leaving him to squint at his note pad. The darkness continued to grow to the point where he couldn't see anything. "Stop it now," he shouted, raising his voice. He couldn't even see the lights from the security cameras, smoke detectors, or the exit signs. His breath caught in his throat. "Damnit, turn the lights on!"

A small area in front of him brightened as if someone shone a flashlight at him.

"Thank you," he called out. "How about passing that over?"

Nobody answered.

He attempted to reach for the flashlight but felt nothing. "What the fuck," he whispered.

"Please, don't be afraid," a masculine voice said from the opposite direction.

Algernon spun around to face the voice. The light followed his movements. "Who said that?" He hoped he didn't sound as spooked as he thought he did.

"You can call me 'M', for conversation's sake, as I wish for my identity to be a mystery, though a man of your talents should have no trouble figuring out who I am."

*I can't place the accent, but it is definitely not American.*

"So, what is this parlor trick, M?" Algernon tried to keep his growing annoyance at bay.

"I assure you that this is no parlor trick. The explanation is lengthy and beyond your comprehension, for now. There, light remains because most people are a little afraid of the dark, no matter what they claim."

Algernon rubbed his hands together, feeling a slight chill. "I'm not quite satisfied with that explanation," he said to M. "What are you doing in my exhibit, M?"

"I wanted to see you alone before I left town. You haven't been alone until now." A little bit of a strange brogue drifted in and out of the stranger's words.

Algernon regained his faculties and considered the words. "See me? What about?"

M emitted a soft sigh. "I've been watching you. We've been watching you for many years, now, Dr. MacDonough. Your work is exemplary. The theories you have about the levels of interactions between the Romans and the Irish Celts are accurate."

"How... how could you know?"

"It was such a shame that the house in Bath had to be abandoned," M continued. "I loved that house. My family loved that house. However, it became too expensive to maintain. Better to let others enjoy it as a museum. I can't believe we left so much behind, though."

"What are you talking about," Algernon asked M.

"But... you found them, Dr. MacDonough. You found the hidden vaults deep within the catacombs. That is a fantastic feat."

Algernon could tell M paced around a bit. The man didn't seem to trip over anything in the dark, yet the shining light revealed nothing of M.

M began speaking again. "We forgot the treasures left behind, at least the treasures of a personal nature. After learning about the exhibit, one of us attended your program and took note of the lost possessions. There were several things that we had to take back, Dr. MacDonough."

He still felt confused.

*How can M talk about these artifacts as if they were his own?*

"Is the fidchell board yours," Algernon asked before he could think over more profound questions. But instead of a receiving vocal answer, he swore he could see two pinpoints of green appear beyond the glow of the white light. Soon, the stress of losing the artifacts began to ebb away.

*I can get out of here and go back to Cheri, soon.*

M finally answered. "I realize you feel that this was the pinnacle of your life's work and that you're very upset we took some of the artifacts back. However, your journey is not over. You have much left to discover. Perhaps you should search for ruins of a great home outside Vézelay. There are so many treasures left in this world." M stopped speaking for a moment, but when he continued, his voice was much closer, as if he spoke into Algernon's ear. "I hope that when you return to your hotel room, your ill feelings toward me and my friends will fade. You have done us a great service, and I thank you for it. I'm certain our paths will cross again, Dr. MacDonough."

Serenity surrounded Algernon, and all became silent. After a few moments, Algernon called out, "M? M," but that voice did not reply. At that moment, the lights started illuminating the exhibit hall again. Everything seemed to be normal, and he knew himself to be alone. Algernon looked around one more time, just to confirm nothing else was missing. Thankfully, the rest of the exhibit were still there.

He exhaled, realizing that no one other than him remained in the hall. Algernon took one last look around the room and decided to leave the museum. He walked quickly through the doors, waved at security, and raced to the exit to find a cab.

Algernon walked into his room at the hotel feeling rather silly.

*I probably imagined the entire experience. Damn Winston's horrible coffee.*

Then he noticed a package on the bed.

*What's this?*

Algernon found his breath again.

*Fear is absolutely useless.*

He reasoned that the unsealed box could contain anything. Algernon moved to the bed and pulled the box open. He stared into the box and inhaled. He heard and felt a squeak in the back of his throat upon seeing what was inside. He couldn't tell if he should be excited or frightened that the open box contained a Roman general's helm.

*No. This is a joke.*

He removed the pillowcase from his pillow to use as makeshift gloves and removed the headgear from the box. His earlier belief that it had to be a toy or prop faded. He could see his own reflection in the metal. At first glance, he believed the style would be older than the majority of the items in the exhibit. Algernon scoffed at his naiveté.

*This has to be a movie prop, a very well-made movie prop.*

Then he noticed a note at the bottom of the box.

*1 Roman General's helm circa 55 B.C.E. as attested by M.G.P.H.*

Algernon nearly dropped the artifact. A hand-written note fluttered to the carpet, revealing map coordinates in France. It was signed 'M'.

Algernon grabbed his cellphone, while continuing to grip the helm with the pillowcase.

"Pick up, Cheri," he whispered, before hitting the talk button twice.

Cheri finished parking her Geo and headed to the apartment, noting how brilliant the full moon seemed tonight. After unlocking and opening the front door, Morty bounded off the couch to greet her.

Sophia looked up from her paperwork. "No, Algernon hasn't called, yet," Sophia preemptively said with a smirk, "but Mort has been whining for you, and wondering why you didn't call."

Cheri dumped her stuff and picked up Morty. "Awww, has mom's lil' man actually missed her?" She grinned while rubbing the cat. "Sorry I didn't call. I was grading and wanted to see if anything new would come in."

*Sorry to lie to you... I was just passing the time, waiting for Algernon's return.*

"Well, you missed a lot of excitement here," Sophia announced before taking off her glasses.

"Really?" Cheri sat down in the recliner.

"Norm came by with that cutie of his to drop off a homemade pie for us. I'm pretty sure you wanna share that pie with me, don't you?" Sophia's smile brightened. "Oh yeah, there's another delivery for you."

"Really?" Cheri smiled back at her roommate. "What is it?"

"I don't know. It's in a box."

"Oh, I was sorta hoping for flowers."

*I can't remember the last time I received flowers.*

"Well, it wasn't delivered by a package delivery company," Sophia added. "Some woman dropped it off. She was dressed very well for a delivery girl. Gorgeous, too."

Cheri considered that for a moment. "What did she look like?"

"I... don't remember, but she said her name was M... something. Eh, I must have forgotten it. My brain is fried, apparently," Sophia stated. "It's on your bed."

"So, want some pie?" Cheri asked Sophia. "I'm a mite peckish."

"So am I, and it's got all sorts of berries in it," Sophia called out, before heading for the kitchen.

Cheri entered her bedroom, with Mort following her, and examined the unsealed box, which seemed to be decent-sized. As she pulled down the flaps, Morty ducked his chin over a side to look in the box. She recognized a wooden block with grooves and grinned. She pulled out a modern fidchell set, which, though modern, still managed to be breathtaking. "Who sent this to me?"

"That's a really pretty present," Sophia responded while leaning into her room. "What is it?"

"It's a fidchell board," she informed Sophia. "It's like a Celtic form of chess."

Sophia entered the room. "Is there more in the box," she asked.

Cheri glanced back in the box. "Yeah, I see some other things." She found a leather scroll case and opened it. She held it over the bed and shook it. A thumb drive and several laminated sheets joined it on her unmade bed. She started thumbing through the pages.

"Ahem?" Sophia grinned.

"It's some old German, I think," Cheri answered. "Then something that looks Gaelic, maybe. I don't know, really. I need an expert to study these." She then saw a small wooden box and pulled it out.

Morty began to investigate the scrolls, but Cheri pulled him away. "Oh no you don't," she said as she put the cat on the floor. However, a few seconds later, he leapt directly into the box and started to scratch the interior. She stared in awe at the intricate carved box, ignoring Mort's flying fur. She opened the wooden box and found a tarot deck within, which was titled 'Otherworld'. "I've never heard of the Otherworld deck," Cheri murmured. She flipped through it and found pictures of various beings of classical, Celtic, and other mythologies. She inhaled, wanting to cry over its' beauty. "This is the most beautiful deck I've ever seen." As she started, it almost seemed as if the images came to life, but she chalked it up to some cheesy holographic effects.

"There's a note," Sophia chimed in, breaking Cheri's enthrallment.

"What," Cheri asked her roommate.

"I saw the envelope and I wanted to... I'm sorry. I thought if it was something from Algernon, I figured I'd call you right away. I hope you don't mind," Sophia said.

"What does it say," Cheri asked. She placed the tarot deck back in the box and closed it.

Sophia grabbed the card on Cheri's shelf and began to read it. "I know you loved my fidchell board, so I hope you'll accept this as a replacement. I was asked to include these scrolls so you could learn their meaning and pass down the knowledge. Oh, we understand that you are fond of Tarot decks. This set is a one of a kind, at least in this world. Enjoy the gifts. Farewell for now. M." Sophia put down the note. "Oh, I get it, sorta. M is Algernon," she said with a chuckle. "That's very cute."

"I've gotta call Algernon." She didn't know whether she should be worried or excited.

*No, this has to be Algernon.*

"Fine," Sophia said as she patted Cheri's shoulder. "I'll heat up the pie. Don't worry, sweetie."

Cheri grabbed the cell phone in order to dial his number, but to her surprise, her phone lit up. It was Algernon calling her. She hit talk, put the phone to her ear, and said, "Algernon?"

"Cheri," Algernon greeted.

"That was way better than flowers," she said, smiling, though she was confused why he talked over her, excited about something... something along the lines of 'you'll never believe who I spoke to.'

"What," they asked in unison. "Who?"

# about the authors

*Heather Poinsett Dunbar*

Born in Houston, Texas, Heather began writing her first book at age eight. While her grammatical structure left much to be desired, she continued to hone her writing and storytelling skills. During a college internship in London, England, her curiosity about ancient cultures and mythology intensified. She backpacked through Europe, fell in love with Scotland, cried at the retelling of part of the Ulster cycle, garnered ghost stories from the Beefeaters at the Tower, wandered the Roman ruins in Bath, and danced around the stones in Avebury.

After spending all her spare time studying these new interests in many libraries and on the road, she began working on her masters' in Library and Information Science at the University of North Texas. She now resides in the Houston area with her husband and three cats. She loves exploring the local culture as well as the many Celtic festivals and events in Texas. She also works as a librarian for a local college, and her favorite authors include Morgan Llewellyn, Neil Gaiman, Terry Pratchett, Evelyn Vaughn, Alison Weir, and Randy Lee Eickhoff.

*Christopher Dunbar*

Chris Dunbar was born in Greenport, Long Island, New York and then moved to Texas as soon as he could, at least that is the story he tells to native Texans, such as his wife. Chris keeps searching for ways to leave Houston, like moving to Auburn, Alabama, Dallas, and even San Antonio, but Houston just keeps reeling him back. Chris' day job is performing Business Continuity and Disaster Recovery, but his night job is coming up with creative ways to wound and maim the characters he and his wife Heather created. For fun, Chris enjoys the occasional novel and video game, but he also likes to delve into his Scottish ancestry and tool leather. When he can find the time, Chris pretends to play the Bodhran and the didgeridoo, much to the chagrin of his cats, Clyde, Brigid, and Lily, not to mention his wife Heather. Chris is also an avid wearer of the kilt.

# published and future works

| Title | Synopsis |
|---|---|
| *Morrigan's Brood*<br>Morrigan's Brood Book I | Éire is invaded by a race of blood-drinkers seeking an artifact they believe will restore them to power. Yet the Deargh Du, the protectors of Éire, are not prepared to defend the island. Only with the help of a Roman general from an earlier time can they hope to rise up against the invaders. |
| *Rise of the Lamia*<br>A Story of the Morrigan's Brood Series | After being freed from his Irish prison in the trees, Marcus Gallerius Primus Helveticus infiltrates the Lamia in Rome on a mission to prevent Emperor Caligula from invating Brittain. Yet his "friend" Mandubratius, a fledgling Lamia, stands in his way. Will Marcus or his nemesis prevail? |
| *Crone of War*<br>Morrigan's Brood Book II | The Lamia expeditionary force has gained a foothold in Éire and has formed an alliance with a powerful Irish chieftain and his malevolent mother. To reinforce them, a massive Lamia army, which is departing Rome, will soon give them enough power to conquer Éire and find their lost treasure. Will the Deargh Du and their new-found friends be able to protect Éire from the invaders, or will the Deargh Du's suspicion of other blood-drinkers allow their enemies to be victorious? |
| *Madness*<br>Short-Story | Following the events of 564 CE, madness strikes one of the Lamia's most important personages. Can the Lamia march on, or will this insanity cast them into civil war? |
| *Reckoning*<br>Short-Story | Following the events of 564 CE, the Deargh Du must come to grips with change or see old strife resurface, which could tear the Deargh Du apart. |
| *Dark Alliance*<br>Morrigan's Brood Book III | A new menace threatens the Balance within the Holy Roman Empire as vicious murders of both mortals and blood-drinkers spread throughout the empire like wildfire. Can a hastily formed alliance between archenemies thwart this new menace, or will festering hatred bring about the empire's doom? |
| *Curse of Venus*<br>Morrigan's Brood Book IV | The Strigoi, the Cursed of Venus, have spread through the Holy Roman Empire and parts beyond like a plague. In response, Pope Leo III takes advantage of the scourge to settle an old score with the man he placed on the throne: Charlemagne. Will their bitter rivalry send the Empire further into chaos and destruction, or will their Deargh Du "angels" save them from themselves and from Venus' Cursed? |
| *Shards of Light*<br>Morrigan's Brood Book V | Many sets of eyes peer through the mist, watching events unfold as the dark alliance seeks out an ancient device that they hope will uncorrupt the menace that has nearly brought the Holy Roman Empire to its knees. However, not everyone beyond the mist is content merely to watch. |
| *Dynasties of Night*<br>Morrigan's Brood Book VI | For centuries, two game masters, a brother and sister, have sat in front of the most intricate game imaginable and watched as the events they set in motion played out. At the forefront of this game are two dynasties of long-lived blood-drinkers: the Kyonshi of Japan, who, like their mortal brethren, strive for independence from China, and the Chiang-shih of China, who wish to maintain control of Japan and the Kyonshi. Will the masters continue to watch the game unfold, or will greed, jealousy, and vengeance bring about an end to this long-running game? |
| *Odin's Chosen*<br>Morrigan's Brood Book VII | Odin hears the call of a proud king unable to feed his starving people and grants him an unusual gift: immortality. Fueled by the need for vengeance against those who murdered his warriors and condemned his people to starvation, Runolf, the new King of Odin's Chosen, leads his fledgling army of blood-drinkers in a war against Britain, Scotland, and Ireland. Little does he know that other races of blood-drinkers inhabit these lands... among them, the Deargh Du. How can Morrigan's Brood hope to maintain the balance when they are at the heart of Runolf's rampage? |

| Title | Synopsis |
| --- | --- |
| **_Hera's Wrath_**<br><br>Morrigan's Brood Book VIII | Many old, dark horrors lie imprisoned in realms unknown to mortal man. In one of these places outside of space and time sleeps a race of voracious eaters cast out of the world by the Tuatha dé Danann, the Gods and Goddesses of Éire. However, every prison has its keys, and Hera, Greek Goddess of Motherhood and Home possess most of them. Will Hera ransom the keys for a return to proper Greek family values, or will she unleash these dark horrors upon mortal man? |
| **_It's In the Cards_**<br><br>A Lusty Librarian Adventure | Cheri (not Cherry) has everything going for her... an over-protective mother who only wants the best for her socially awkward daughter, an overly needy would-be boyfriend, and a dream job in the basement of some college library... wait, she actually likes the job. Life for her is... mediocre?... meh, until a professor named Algernon and a strange collection of rare artifacts enter her life, and then the fabric of the universe changes forever. Well, not really; she just has fun, for once in her life. Come, join in her romp. |
| **_Bitches Love Unicorns_**<br><br>Within _Dark Constellation: Origins_, Book 1 of the Dark Constellation Series | Ever been to a wild party, the kind where everyone, including you, is dancing to a fevered pitch, where you meet this gorgeous someone, who is really into you, and it turns out that hot looking person cozying up to you is really a unicorn, which, as a kid, you had fantasized about but you never really thought they were real but hoped they were? Kayleigh discovers the truth, that unicorns do exist, along with a myriad of other fantastical beings, in the Otherworld. Bob the Unicorn sweeps Kayleigh off her feet and whisks her away on a trip through time, space, and magical realms, as the pair keep the party going. But like all things, this party must eventually come to an end. |
| **_Dudes Love Faeries_**<br><br>Within _Dark Constellation: Origins_, Book 1 of the Dark Constellation Series | Ever started a new job only to find your new boss is actually evil incarnate? Enter Teddy, a pixie librarian, who ventures to the realm of the unseelie for what he hopes to be a fulfilling job at the largest and most prestigious library in Tír na nÓg. After proving himself superior to his boss, he is demoted to the lowliest position in the library: book-duster. His new boss, a seemingly inept unseelie with a secret desire to reshape Tír na nÓg for his own gain, accompanies him when they stumble upon long-hidden magical machines deep within the bowels of the library. Teddy soon realizes these machines could change the very fabric of existence in the Otherworld. Good thing his boss, Dathúil, can't read the manual; otherwise, his desires may come to fruition, to the detriment of all. |
| **_One Fat Witch_**<br><br>Book 2 of the Dark Constellation Series | Hazel, Kayleigh's daughter, enjoys a topsy-turvey living in Houston, Texas with two jobs at one of the most mediocre institutions of higher learning in the State of Texas... Professor of Archeology and receptionist (they won't make her a full-time professor, so she has to work the other job to fill out her hours). One night, she and her husband Jack are dining out at a Brazilian steakhouse, when a gunman attacks. Their waiter, a unicorn in human form, rescues Jack and disappears. Hazel seeks the aid of Teddy, the proprietor of a local metaphysical shop, whom she discovers is a pixie hiding in the mortal realm from her pursuer, Dathúil... an unseelie who is attempting to reacquire a key, stolen by Teddy and hidden in the mortal realm. With this key, Dathúil could control the massive magical machines running the Otherworld. Can Hazel find her husband and protect the key, or will the unseelie find his treasure and fulfill his murderous ambitions of total dominion? |

www.ingramcontent.com/pod-product-compliance
Lightning Source LLC
Chambersburg PA
CBHW020619130626
46552CB00003B/1044